Under Fire

"Down!" Charvein threw Lucy down while Sandoval jerked away to the other side. The window shattered and the lantern crashed against the wooden counter behind them, spewing flaming coal oil on the floor.

"Oh, my God!" she screamed.

Flames had splashed Sandoval's poncho, and Charvein tackled him, smothering the fire before the flames could burn through the woven cloth.

"I'm okay," Sandoval gasped, pulling the smoking poncho off over his head.

Lucy was cowering in the corner, pistol in one hand, eyes wide in the light of the flames that were licking up the counter and spreading across the floor.

"Stay down!" Charvein yelled. "Don't make a target." The sudden brightness had blinded him, and he fired through the window with little hope of hitting anyone. He saw muzzle flashes from outside, and bullets smashed the remaining shards of glass that clung to the sash. By the time he and Sandoval returned fire, the flashes had moved, coming closer.

THE SECRET
OF LODESTAR

Tim Champlin

BERKLEY BOOKS, NEW YORK

The Berkley Publishing Group
Published by the Penguin Group
Penguin Group (USA) Inc.
375 Hudson Street, New York, New York 10014, USA

Penguin Group (Canada), 90 Eglinton Avenue East, Suite 700, Toronto, Ontario M4P 2Y3, Canada
(a division of Pearson Penguin Canada Inc.)
Penguin Books Ltd., 80 Strand, London WC2R 0RL, England
Penguin Group Ireland, 25 St. Stephen's Green, Dublin 2, Ireland (a division of Penguin Books Ltd.)
Penguin Group (Australia), 250 Camberwell Road, Camberwell, Victoria 3124, Australia
(a division of Pearson Australia Group Pty. Ltd.)
Penguin Books India Pvt. Ltd., 11 Community Centre, Panchsheel Park, New Delhi—110 017, India
Penguin Group (NZ), 67 Apollo Drive, Rosedale, Auckland 0632, New Zealand
(a division of Pearson New Zealand Ltd.)
Penguin Books (South Africa) (Pty.) Ltd., 24 Sturdee Avenue, Rosebank, Johannesburg 2196,
South Africa

Penguin Books Ltd., Registered Offices: 80 Strand, London WC2R 0RL, England

This is a work of fiction. Names, characters, places, and incidents either are the product of the author's imagination or are used fictitiously, and any resemblance to actual persons, living or dead, business establishments, events, or locales is entirely coincidental. The publisher does not have any control over and does not assume any responsibility for author or third-party websites or their content.

THE SECRET OF LODESTAR

A Berkley Book / published by arrangement with the author

PRINTING HISTORY
Berkley edition / March 2012

ISBN: 978-0-425-24657-3

BERKLEY®
Berkley Books are published by The Berkley Publishing Group,
a division of Penguin Group (USA) Inc.,
375 Hudson Street, New York, New York 10014.
BERKLEY® is a registered trademark of Penguin Group (USA) Inc.
The "B" design is a trademark of Penguin Group (USA) Inc.

PRINTED IN THE UNITED STATES OF AMERICA

10 9 8 7 6 5 4 3 2 1

For Ellie, with love

ONE

Boom!

A big-bore rifle thundered across the baking silence.

Marc Charvein snapped his head left. A puff of white smoke blossomed from the flank of the desert mountain. Suddenly his horse jerked and stumbled forward.

He instinctively kicked his right boot clear of the stirrup, tucked his shoulder, and rolled away as nine hundred pounds of horse went down, thudding into the packed earth. Marc somersaulted, landing on his back, jarring his breath out. Head spinning from the impact, he scrambled up and dove behind his horse's body as the rifle boomed again.

The slug kicked dirt from the spot he'd just vacated. He peeked over the horse's withers, toward the mountainside from where the shots originated. Nothing moved. The only sounds were his own heart slamming softly against his rib cage and a fitful desert wind whispering across the playa, chasing the echoes.

The weathered face of the barren mountain swam in rising heat waves less than a mile away. The sun was too high to throw into relief the creases and gullies in the hillside, where a shooter might be hiding. And Marc couldn't pinpoint where he'd seen the puff of smoke. Nearly twenty years had passed since he was last ambushed—by a war party of Apaches in New Mexico when he was a corporal in the Third Cavalry. But those Indians were not marksmen, and they attacked with an odd assortment of stolen rifles for which they had little ammunition.

Blood trickled from his horse's temple, indicating a fatal head wound. At least it had been mercifully quick. But had the bullet been intended for Marc? Apparently so, or the rifleman wouldn't have fired again so quickly.

From the sound of the shot, and its obvious distance, it had to be a .50-caliber from Denson Boyd's long-barreled Sharps. Marc could visualize the man cursing his miss as he slid another long brass cartridge into the breech of the single-shot rifle, slammed home the shell with the lever, jerked the rifle to his shoulder, and fired without aiming through the vernier sight. The special Sharps was Boyd's signature weapon, one he'd previously used to fend off pursuing posses. Four lawmen trying to close the gap on this man had felt the sting of the big slugs guided by an unerring eye— an eye which never seemed to sleep. More than one posse had decided the wiser course was to return to town with the tale they'd lost Denson Boyd and his gang in the desert mountains.

This was the man Marc Charvein was now trailing— who'd spotted and dry-gulched him. Charvein had made it into the third day of his solo manhunt; he should have known to keep his distance. But he couldn't drop too far back, for fear of losing his quarry altogether. And it was impossible to stay hidden while moving in this barren Nevada desert. Traveling at night, he could do well enough with moon and stars but risked passing Boyd, who would likely camp in some lonely canyon. And riding by day, his horse raised a dust plume that could be seen for miles. To avoid being spotted in open country, he could take to the steep, rocky terrain. But there he'd lose time and run the risk of his horse falling and breaking a leg. So he compromised and rode along the base of the mountains, trying to keep pace with, but not overtake, Denson Boyd. Charvein wasn't trying to catch up—only keep him in sight until Boyd could lead him to the cached loot.

Perhaps Boyd had intended to kill the horse, to set his pursuer afoot in a waterless wilderness, miles from anywhere. After all, Boyd was now legally free and wouldn't want to add murder—a hanging offense—to his lengthy record.

Four years earlier—in June of 1881—Boyd and two others, Martin Stepenaw and Glen Savage, alias the Weasel, had held up a train just outside Gold Hill, Nevada, ambushed and wounded four guards, and blown open the express car, making off with $30,000 in gold ingots being shipped to the Carson City mint.

Two months later they'd gotten drunk and careless in Virginia City. A woman faro dealer alerted the sheriff that Stepenaw had tried to pay her with slivers of metal hacked from a gold bar. He, Boyd, and Savage were arrested, and the damning evidence found on Stepenaw was part of a small ingot still bearing the "O" stamp of the Overstrike Mine. Put on trial with no hope of acquittal, the three were offered a reduced sentence if they'd reveal the location of the stolen treasure. They refused and were sentenced to twenty years in the state prison at Carson.

Though rumored to be the ringleader, Boyd was released after only four years, through the intervention of one man— Ezra Pitney, owner of the stolen gold. It was a generally known secret that Pitney had sweetened the coffers of the

governor's upcoming campaign fund with a sizable contri-
bution in return for the governor commuting Boyd's sentence to time served.

Marc Charvein lay pinned down, Colt in hand but no target in sight. He wondered why the governor had selected this
member of the trio for release. Probably because Boyd was
the smartest and meanest, and Ezra Pitney knew he'd head
straight for the hidden gold. It figured. It also figured that
Boyd would expect to be followed.

Charvein wiped a gloved hand across his brow; the doeskin came away streaked with salt and grime. He ran his
tongue over his dry, cracked lips.

What now? He was in the open without even a clump
of sage or a creosote bush to hide behind. Sucking in a
breath of superheated air, he fervently cursed his luck. On
the baking ground behind his dead horse, he regretted with
all his soul that he'd ever taken Pitney's offer to track this
man and find the mine owner's stolen gold.

He fumbled for his nickel-plated pocket watch. Half past
twelve. He forced himself to lie concealed another half
hour. Was the shooter also patiently waiting, training his
long buffalo gun on the dead horse, assuming Marc would
rise up sooner or later and also become buzzard food? The
thought made him sweat. He tried to put himself in Denson Boyd's mind. If the ex-convict intended to retrieve the
stolen gold—and surely that was the only reason for rush-
ing out into this wilderness with a pack mule—then he had
to discourage any pursuit. For all Boyd knew, Charvein was
just another outlaw. If ever caught and tried for murder,
Boyd could always claim self-defense. There were no witnesses. Who could say otherwise? It would be his word
against a dead man's. More likely, Marc Charvein would
just vanish without a trace, vultures, wolves, and insects

reducing his remains to scattered bones soon concealed by windblown dust and sand. He shivered at the image of his own demise.

But a slow anger ignited. He resolved to take back the offensive. He would not be intimidated. Even though he was out of water, he still had plenty of life in him.

In less than thirty minutes, the flies began to gather, buzzing in the stillness. He rolled onto his back and squinted at the brassy sky from under his bent hat brim. Far above, black vultures soared on rising thermals, drifting silently like charred pieces of paper blown aloft from a fire.

He took a deep breath and exhaled. All parties to this drama bided their time—the shooter, Charvein, and the vultures who waited for the man to abandon the dead horse or become food himself. Death was slow, but vultures were patient. Charvein smiled grimly. They were nature's cleanup squad. It was just such as these that reinforced his belief in God—one part of nature balancing another.

With thoughts like these, he entertained himself in a deliberate attempt to keep his mind off the man with the long-range rifle.

He finally bellied up to the neck of his fallen horse, removed his hat, and raised one eye above the body, hoping the shooter wasn't constantly alert, trigger finger ready. Marc wished for his field glasses to scan the gray hillside. But they lay, probably crushed, in the saddlebags beneath his dead horse. The silence was maddening. How much longer should he wait, ignoring his thirst and the sun that was sucking him dry? The only safe thing to do was wait until cover of darkness, but that was still many hours away.

What would he do if he were in Boyd's position? "Hell, if I'd been behind the wall four years, I'd just set any pursuer afoot, then move on. Let the desert finish the job," he muttered to himself. *Killing my horse, he thinks he's killed me. He won't waste any more time here; he'll take off after that gold.*

He placed his hat on the barrel of his Colt and eased it above the animal's body. He moved it around slightly, but it drew no fire. "The bastard's gone," he grunted. "Time for me to go, too."

Sucking in a deep breath, he crawled around to the other side of his horse. The body was bloating and the cinch was tight, so he took his sheath knife and slashed the webbing and the surcingle. Returning to the top of the saddle, he gripped the horn and the cantle, placed a foot on either side and tugged until his breath became raspy and sweat stung his eyes. "Damned stirrup is hanging it up." He wiggled the saddle from side to side until he finally managed to drag it free from the soft dirt under the horse. The rifle in its scabbard was dirty but undamaged. The three-quart cloth-covered canteen was another matter. The neck, with the stopper inserted, had been broken off, spilling all the water.

"Shit!" Charvein exploded. "Needed this more than the rifle." But at least the container wasn't crushed. He'd conserved that water, not drinking any for the last eighteen hours, only rinsing his mouth now and then before spitting it back into the metal canteen. He'd been down to three good swallows, so the loss was not great.

He rummaged in the topside saddlebag, took out a rag, some oil and a cleaning rod, and gave the rifle a thorough cleaning. The new Colt Lightning pump used the same .44-40 cartridges as his revolver. He had two boxes of fifty cartridges each, plus what was in the magazine. He struggled to drag the rest of the saddlebags out from under the horse. They held a change of clothes and a few strips of beef jerky. He was hungry, but he left the jerky alone until he found some water; the dried beef would only serve to make him even thirstier.

He stood and scanned the horizon, noting that he was in a wide valley between two low ranges of mountains that jutted up sharply like the broken teeth of a crosscut saw. Somewhere within those gun-sight notches and hidden canyons might be springs or seeps of water. But he couldn't bet on it this time of year. The terrain matched hundreds of other places in Nevada. Rows of mountains ran mostly northwest to southeast, with wide, flat valleys between. And the distances were vast, dwarfing humans. There were not even any life-sustaining, moisture-hoarding barrel cactus or prickly pear such as those in the Sonoran Desert far to the south. Nevada was what he pictured the surface of the moon to be—lifeless rocks and jagged mountains and dust— plenty of dust—baked by a merciless sun. Even Indians avoided places like this that wouldn't even sustain plants.

He pulled out his watch and wound it out of habit. The only time that mattered here was daylight and dark and the long rhythms of nature.

He slung the saddlebags over his left shoulder, hooked the strap of the empty canteen over his right, gripped the rifle, and started walking west by south. Instinct told him there would not be another ambush. Boyd, riding a mule and trailing another with a pack saddle, was likely several miles ahead by now, but going in which direction? Only God, or the devil, knew.

Charvein tried not to think of his predicament. Except for Boyd, there probably wasn't another human within a hundred miles. He'd angle across toward the nearest range of mountains several miles distant, so he could slip into the canyons an hour or so before dark and hunt for water, pos- sibly tracking prints of a coyote or some smaller desert critters to a seep or tank. Fresh-flowing streams were out of the question.

It was a desperate gamble. He was far from being a tracker or skilled outdoorsman.

Before him a waterless lake bed stretched for miles, streaked here and there with white deposits. The crusty surface was cracked into millions of pieces like a brown mosaic. A shimmering veil of heat made the distant mountains weave in some macabre dance. Wind devils spun across the surface, whirling dust hundreds of feet into the air in columns like small tornadoes. Charvein watched these whirlwinds. Some appeared to stand still; others moved slowly, gradually dissipating while others formed.

This part of the world received only a few inches of rain a year, and often it came in two or three violent storms, hours apart.

Marc wondered what this area looked like after one of those storms. Consistent with the nature of this land, the rain would not be a gentle soaker. Hard downpours with lightning and thunder—male rain—would transform the low-lying surface into a shimmering lake, several inches to a foot deep.

But the dominant sun always returned to suck up the moisture. And what didn't evaporate sank beneath the surface.

The wind picked up, blowing directly into his face. Sand stung his exposed skin. He paused and removed the bandanna from his neck and tied it around his mouth and nose. Tugging down his hat brim, he bent his head and trudged on, the empty canteen banging against his hip, the rifle in one hand, saddlebags dragging at his left shoulder.

The afternoon wore on. Dust coated him. His squinted eyes became irritated from grit. The wind gusted stronger, scouring the playa, throwing clouds of dust into the air.

Using the pale disk of sun, he held his direction. But when it finally dropped behind the distant mountains and the atmosphere grew murkier with advancing nightfall, he could no longer be sure.

As the hours of darkness dragged, he became disoriented. How wide was this playa? There was no way to tell if he was lost and walking in circles, because wind and dust filled in or wiped out his tracks in the soft crust.

Suddenly he stumbled when his weight broke through the crusted mud and he sank over his ankles into a slushy liquid. Off balance, he struggled forward, trying not to fall as he dragged his boots through the slop. He knew the water, saturated with salts, was not drinkable. Maybe he could just moisten his tongue. He yanked down the bandanna, reached and wet his gloved fingers, and put them to his tongue. Bitter. The undrinkable liquid stung his cracked lips. He spat. What a hell he'd wandered into! He had thought he'd reach the mountains before dark, but distances were deceiving in this dry air. Perhaps the mountains contained *tinajas*—tanks of stagnant rainwater cupped in hollows scoured out of solid rock by rain and sandstorms over eons.

He dragged his boots out of the muck and trudged onward, blindly, numbly, thinking of nothing. Time and distance had ceased to mean anything. The wind gusted in his face so strongly he could lean against it. The bottoms of his feet burned through the cotton socks and thin leather soles. At least his boots prevented the alkalai from reaching his blistered skin.

Thirst grew so compelling that he paused, turned his back to the wind, and urinated into the empty canteen. Cringing, he tipped it up and drank. It wasn't much and it was warm and salty, but it relieved the dryness of his tongue and throat. At a bare minimum, it required a gallon of water a day for a man to survive in this place. And even that might not be enough. God! What a way to die. He envisioned a future traveler stumbling across his bleached and scattered bones, skull grinning at some cosmic joke.

Death would come within a day or so. But death would be better than being eternally damned to a place that not even Dante had described. But then, Dante had never seen Nevada.

He opened the flap of the saddlebags and took out the two heavy boxes of cartridges and shoved them and the jerky into the pockets of his jeans. Then he dropped the bags containing the crushed field glasses, currycomb, his extra clothing, razor, and soap. Somewhat lightened, he trudged on, carrying the canteen, his rifle and belted six-gun. In his growing weakness, he considered discarding one of his weapons. The only enemies he'd likely encounter out here were not ones he could oppose with bullets.

The deep dryness of thirst entered its next stage, where the nerve endings of his skin felt scraped and irritated by the rubbing of his clothing—as if he'd been sprinkled with sand. His mind wandered, and he lost focus and awareness. Hallucinations would follow.

He stumbled where the ground rose slightly under his feet, jolting him back to the present. Several more steps brought him up from the soft, sandy surface onto something more solid. Had he finally reached the end of the playa?

A strange noise arrested his attention. He paused, swaying with fatigue, the gusting wind like a chorus of rising and falling voices. Then the sharp noise again. The gong of a bell? Impossible! He strained to hear, cocking his head this way and that. "Imagining things. A ringing in your ears, you fool," he tried to say aloud, but it was only a thought since his swollen tongue and dry lips prevented speech. *An angel coming to greet me?* A sardonic grin cracked his lower lip and he grimaced. Surely the devil didn't ring a bell to announce his arrival.

Then he heard it again—not the tinkle of a small chime, such as a goat might wear around its neck, but more like the light, mellow tone of a big brass bell. He was convinced he'd actually heard it, and he staggered on unsteady legs toward the sound, like a crippled ship blindly seeking a bell buoy in a harbor. Real or imagined, the metallic sound lured him on—not a rhythmic ring, but only a dim, sporadic *bong* . . . *bong* . . .

He grew light-headed and dizzy. Suddenly his limbs went limp, and he felt himself falling into a black hole.

TWO

Marc Charvein burst awake, drowning. He jerked upright, strangling, sputtering, spraying water from nose and mouth.

"Easy!" a voice said.

"Huh . . . ?" He cringed away, still hacking to clear his throat. His tongue and lips were wet, and he managed to swallow.

"Here," the stranger said, thrusting a blanket-sided canteen into Charvein's hand.

He tipped it up and poured the cool, clear, life-giving liquid into his mouth and swallowed and swallowed. He couldn't get enough.

"Bastante!" A strong hand snatched the canteen, sloshing water onto his shirt. "Enough for now."

"More," he gasped. Charvein strained to see his benefactor, but irritated eyes could make out only a darker shadow in the dust-blurred moonlight.

A hand reached under his arm and pulled him to his feet. He was as weak and wobbly as a newborn colt. "My rifle?" His holster was also empty.

The unseen arm was guiding him, and he followed meekly, unable to do otherwise. With a start, he realized the bulky shapes around him were buildings. He'd stumbled into a town. But everyone must be asleep; there were no lights. He had no idea of the time.

"Who are you?" he croaked, his voice sounding like that of some stranger. "Where am I?" Was this a dream of his fevered mind? The specter did not speak, would not answer.

Marc shuffled along the dirt street, a sinewy hand gripping him by the elbow. Buildings on either side protested at being kept from slumber—timbers were creaking, shutters banging, a loose sheet of tin roofing rattled violently.

He longed for more water, craved it with all his dried-up being. He would follow this man wherever he led as long as he could get hold of that canteen again.

They walked at least a half mile while the wind seemed to tire itself out. It still gusted fitfully but was beginning to lose much of its force. Charvein looked up at the waning moon. It appeared to glow inside a dusty halo.

The strange man was leading him toward the bulky flank of a mountain that jutted up close to the last buildings on the street. They stepped through a thick clump of mesquite, and Charvein caught sight of a small fire of coals within the shelter of a cleft in the steep hillside.

"Sit," the voice commanded, motioning toward the fire, where a blanket was spread. The man added a handful of dry sticks to the glowing coals, and Marc looked away from the sudden brightness as they blazed up. He collapsed, loose-limbed, onto the blanket and gazed at his benefactor, who was finally visible. Shorter than average, the man wore a light cotton poncho and a wide straw hat he shoved back to hang by its cord down his back. Longish salt-and-pepper hair swept back to frame a lean, shaven face. Shaven? Marc could see no trace of whiskers on the smooth, leathery

cheeks. The thin, hawklike nose and reddish glow of his
skin in the firelight hinted at a heritage more Indian than
Spanish. Recalling the strength of those tapered fingers,
Charvein assumed the slight figure was strung together with
lean, whipcord muscle. Black eyes gazed at him from under
hooded lids. Charvein shivered in the heat. Dressed a little
differently, this apparition could have just stepped from an
Inca temple to confront the Spanish conquistadors.

"Water."

"*Un poco*," the man replied, tossing the canteen to
Charvein.

This time he managed to discipline himself, rinsing his
dry mouth and swollen tongue before swallowing. He repeated the procedure three times, then forced himself to
cork the vessel. He placed it beside him on the blanket instead of handing it back.

"There is more," the man said.

Good. He spoke English.

"Where am I?" Marc asked when his throat and tongue
felt lubricated enough to speak.

"Lodestar, Nevada," the man said.

"Lodestar . . . ," Marc said, searching his memory. The
silver boomtown of the 1860s, long abandoned. "And who
are you?"

"Sandoval. Baptized 'Carlos,' but no one knows me by
that name."

"An old, honorable Spanish surname."

"The name of one of the Spanish dogs who conquered
the Incan empire three hundred years ago."

"You carry a long hate. You don't appear old enough to
have been there."

"I carry a mix of Incan and Spanish blood."

"Nearly everyone is a mixture of something. Did you
inherit nothing from the Spanish besides their seed?"

"My belief in the one, true God."

"Then consider yourself fortunate."

"Who are you and why are you in Lodestar?" Sandoval asked, ignoring the comment.

"Marchal Charvein—Marc." He uncorked the canteen for another swig. "It's a long story."

"I have time, Marchal Charvein." He paused. "That is a French name," he added.

"Correct. But I'm third generation American. And I don't hate the English for all the wars between France and England. Past hurts to ancestors are best forgotten. You and I are but a short time on this earth."

"Your time was almost very short if I had not found you just now." His speech carried only a slight hint of a Spanish accent. The voice was husky, as if it hadn't been used for a long time, or as if his throat was irritated by dust.

Marc nodded. He pegged Sandoval as eccentric but not dangerous. He owed his benefactor an explanation. "I was hired to find a man who robbed a train near Virginia City and made off with a load of gold ingots. The rightful owner wants it back."

As he hunkered on the opposite side of the dying fire, Sandoval's expression didn't change.

Charvein finished his tale of being ambushed and wandering across the playa.

"Do you have any proof of what you tell me?"

"Do I need any?"

Sandoval gazed at him silently.

Charvein reached into his shirt pocket and drew out a wrinkled, sweat-stained letter he carried from Ezra Pitney verifying that he'd hired Charvein, a former lawman, to find his gold. Marc handed over the letter, along with a worn silver badge and a card signed by the county sheriff in Virginia City appointing him a temporary deputy for one year.

Sandoval looked at the written documents so briefly Marc wondered if the man could read English. He handed them back. "Why do you carry a badge?"

"I'm deputized to make arrests if I need to. I was a full-time railroad detective some years ago." When Sandoval didn't reply, he added, "There are better ways to make a living. I'm still looking for one." He started to grin, but a sharp sting reminded him of his cracked lips. He had to gain Sandoval's confidence so the Mexican would return his weapons. He wiped the copious tears overflowing his irritated eyes. Most of the dust had been washed away.

Sandoval took a short board and scraped the coals of the fire to one side. "You have not eaten."

"I ate two days ago."

The man uncovered the lid of a pot buried in coals beneath the fire. He lifted the lid with a small iron hook. The steaming aroma of cooking beans wafted to Marc's nose, causing his stomach to grumble.

"They are ready."

"You were cooking beans in the middle of the night?"

"*Mañana*," he replied. "My food for tomorrow. But already it is tomorrow. Dawn comes in two hours."

Charvein had lost all sense of time, but he noted that the roaring wind was now only a light breeze fanning the mesquite bushes shielding the entrance to the cave.

Sandoval set the lid to one side, rummaged in a wooden box behind him, pulling out two tin plates, cups, and spoons. He scooped up a generous helping and handed the plate to Charvein. He dished up his own food and sat, cross-legged, on the ground to eat.

"I did not expect company, so I have no bacon or tortillas prepared," Sandoval said.

As they ate, Charvein wondered what this man was doing, living in a town vacated for nearly ten years. During the War Between the States, Lodestar had boomed with silver strikes, even as the Washoe area of western Nevada was developing the mines that would eventually result in the Big Bonanza discoveries of the mid-seventies.

Charvein finished eating and set his plate down. Though still hungry, he dared not push his body, for fear of getting sick.

"Why are you living in a ghost town?" he asked, hoping to catch Sandoval off guard and elicit an honest answer. He didn't succeed.

"It is enough for you to know I'm here and saved you from turning into the dust of this place."

"Then tell me—where do you get food and water? You didn't grow these beans."

"Verdad." Sandoval scraped up the last of the juice with his spoon. "When I need supplies, I ride to Virginia City. I have a mule and a burro."

Apparently, the animals were sheltered somewhere else. "What about water?"

"When the shafts reached fifteen hundred feet, the miners struck water. Flooded all the tunnels. The pumps couldn't lift it out fast enough. The miners could no longer reach the heavy, blue-gray mud that was the silver ore. Without the silver, the town died." He shrugged at the finality of it. "Now the town is mine." A hint of smile crossed his face. "Some of the underground water was ruined by quicksilver and other chemicals. But not all. I found a shaft that contains only cold, pure water—better than any in Nevada."

"I see."

Sandoval packed a blackened pipe with coarse tobacco. He looked up as he touched a blazing twig to the bowl and puffed it to life. "My only vice since I quit drinking mescal."

Although Charvein smoked an occasional cigar, he felt
no desire for tobacco now. His mouth and throat still suffered from extreme dryness.

"What will you do?" Sandoval asked.

"I have lost the robber for the moment. Now I'll try to
pick up his trail or return to Virginia City."

"How will you do this on foot?"

"I was hoping I could use or buy one of your animals."

"Lupida and Jeremiah are my friends, my family. They
are not for sale or rent."

"Then it appears I'm at your mercy." Charvein doubted
he could survive afoot in the mountains, even with all the
water he could carry. Game would also be scarce.

"Perhaps you can ride to Virginia City on my spare
beast—next time I go."

Charvein didn't want to push the tentative offer. "How
far is it from here?"

"Two days' slow ride."

Charvein nodded. Evidently, Sandoval wasn't wanted
by the law in Virginia City. No telling when he was due to
make another run for supplies. *I could be stuck here for
weeks.* "What about my guns?"

Sandoval eyed him sharply, hesitating. Then he reached
under his poncho and withdrew a Colt, handing it over, butt
first. "Your rifle is near where I found you."

Charvein shoved the Colt into its holster, assuming it
had been unloaded.

Water and then hot food, along with his earlier ordeal,
were all having their effect on him, and he felt his eyelids
growing heavy. "Thank you for saving my life," he said and
bowed slightly with a formal courtesy. "And for your hos-
pitality. But now I have to sleep."

"The livery stable still has much dry hay," Sandoval said.
"I'll show you."

He got up and led the still weak Charvein out of their partial shelter and back toward the main street.

The abandoned buildings were now dimly visible in the graying light of approaching dawn. The air still smelled of dust, but the wind had died with the night.

"I remember hearing a bell just before I blacked out," Charvein said. "It led me here."

"From the church of San Juan—that stone building over there." He pointed. "A strong wind can ring the brass bell. When I first came here, I climbed the bell tower to muffle the clapper. But the rotten wood of the stairs collapsed, and I almost broke my leg. Some night, in a great windstorm, it will come crashing down. Meanwhile, the sound has become a companion, like my animals." He turned to Charvein. "Think on that sound as a miracle from San Juan, guiding you to safety."

Was his tone more mocking than pious? Charvein couldn't tell.

"Does the wind always blow at night like that?"

"No. Only in spells."

"Strange."

"The heavy wind blows from the southwest through a canyon in this range of mountains. Something in the bend of the canyon and the rock formations makes the winds howl like a tortured ghost. The Paiutes believe it is the spirit world calling. The Lodestar residents used to call it Nightwind Canyon."

Sandoval detoured to the boardwalk in front of a store, retrieved Charvein's rifle, and handed it to him. Charvein knew without looking that it was empty.

A half block farther brought them to the partially collapsed stable.

"You will not need a light now," Sandoval said, pointing. "The ladder to the loft is sturdy if you want to rake down fresh hay." He turned and walked away without another word.

Charvein, relishing his solitude, made himself a comfortable nest in the corner, wondering if he might be sharing his bed with mice or rats. But he didn't care, as he pulled off his boots and ruined socks and massaged his sore feet, wishing he had some alcohol to douse the three small blisters he found.

He reloaded both his rifle and pistol from his cartridge belt and placed the weapons within easy reach before he curled up in the hay. It was like sleeping on a cloud.

Two hours later he was deep in exhausted sleep and didn't hear the hooves clopping along the street outside.

THREE

"Marc!"

Charvein's eyes flew open at the urgent whisper of his name. He found his mouth firmly clamped with a calloused hand and Sandoval's dark face above him.

"Sshhh!" He pointed toward the street. Sandoval removed his hand, and Charvein carefully reached for his gunbelt, then crept barefoot toward the wall of the stable, where he applied his eye to a crack between the warped boards.

Two mules stood tethered to a sagging hitching rail across the street. MINERS' EXCHANGE BANK was engraved in the stone lintel over the open double doors. From within came the hollow clumping of boots on a wooden floor.

"Your man?" Sandoval whispered.

Charvein nodded, eyeing the stock of the rifle protruding from an overlong scabbard on the riding mule. He knew of only one man in this day of lightweight repeating rifles who carried a long-barreled, heavy Sharps like that. It was the man he was certain had ambushed him—Denson Boyd.

But what was he doing? Was the gold stashed inside that abandoned bank? How ironic!

Half a minute later Boyd stepped out onto the boardwalk, put his hands on his hips, and looked up and down the street. Then he stretched his arms over his head. "YEEE-HAWW!!" he roared, his bellow echoing off the empty buildings.

Charvein glanced at Sandoval, whose dark eyes remained expressionless.

Had Boyd gone mad in this vast desert with only the mules and wind for company? Charvein guessed it was a shout of exuberance or frustration, but he couldn't tell which. If the man had found the stolen gold, he didn't have any of it in his hands. Maybe he was just letting off steam after being unexpectedly freed from prison.

Boyd stepped down to his riding mule, detached a canteen, and tipped it up to drain the last few swallows.

Charvein's hand went to the butt of his Colt. He could take this man into custody right now. But for what? As far as he knew, Boyd had committed no crime, broken no law since he had been released from prison. He wasn't even in possession of stolen gold—yet. Small bags of thick canvas were tied to the empty pack saddle. As they watched, Boyd loosed the mules and led them away down the street. He stopped at one of the town pumps and tried to work it, but the rusted handle wouldn't move. He muttered under his breath and then led the mules down a side street and out of sight.

"Where's he headed now?" Charvein muttered, sitting down to tug his boots onto his bare feet.

"Probably to find water," Sandoval guessed. "There's a stream in the bottom of Nightwind Canyon, but it's dry most of the year."

"Let's get out of here." Charvein grabbed his rifle, and

Sandoval led the way carefully past the collapsed back wall
of the stable. They crept behind the row of stores, saloons,
and a theater, until they reached the end of the dusty thor-
oughfare. A worn tin sign, fastened by rusty nails to the
side of a corner building, identified this as Center Street—
doubtless named by some Lodestar founder who lacked
imagination. The town was larger than Charvein had realized, extending five blocks, with several cross streets.

They finally arrived at the cleft in the hillside where
they'd eaten the night before. So skillfully had Sandoval
scuffed out all evidence, Charvein could hardly tell anyone
had been here. To his surprise, the cleft where they'd eaten
opened up into a spacious chamber, fifteen by twenty feet
and seven feet high, with a packed dirt floor. A burro and a
mule, with feed bags over their muzzles, looked up curiously as the two men entered. Apparently Sandoval, or
someone before him, had excavated an old mine tunnel,
turning this into a snug living quarters. Boxes of supplies
were stacked around the walls—even a few sacks of oats to
supplement the animals' sparse grazing.

"Do any of those other town pumps work?" Charvein
asked.

"No. The ones that aren't rusted have no suction. Leather
pistons are rotted out." When Sandoval squatted beside a
fire ring of dead ashes, his cotton poncho swung outward,
and Charvein noticed a gleaming blue-black Colt revolver
thrust under his belt. It looked to be a popular open-
top, .36-caliber Navy model, converted to fire cartridges. A
Henry rifle stood against the cave wall. The well-kept appearance of the weapons indicated this man was prepared
to hold his own against man or beast.

"No fire until he's gone," Sandoval said, nodding toward
the town. He lifted a blackened coffeepot from the iron
spiderweb and filled two tin cups. "Warm barley coffee—

until my next trip to town," he explained, handing one of the cups to Charvein. "What is your next move?" he asked, calmly sipping the brew.

"Watch where he goes and what he does, but stay out of sight. And you have to keep your animals quiet."

"All our tracks will be blown away, but my animals have left manure."

Charvein bit his lip. "Can't be helped. With those piles dusted over, maybe he'll think the manure is old."

"I'll cover your back," Sandoval offered.

Charvein drained the cup of strange-tasting barley coffee, then took up his rifle. "I can handle this. Thanks for everything you've done for me. If he pulls out of town, I might have to ask for your help to follow."

Sandoval nodded.

Charvein grabbed a canteen hanging on a hook, uncorked it, and took a long drink.

"There is plenty of good water at the end of that tunnel," Sandoval said, pointing at a dark opening that led off the cavern.

"Thanks." It was a relief not to have to conserve.

Rifle in hand, Charvein went outside through the screening brush and cat-footed along the flank of the mountain, taking advantage of every building and shed for concealment as he approached Center Street.

From a distance, he could see the mules now tied in front of a saloon.

A two-story hotel stood across the street from the saloon. Being careful not to kick any rusted cans or trip over any loose boards, Charvein found an outside stairway to the second floor of the hotel and crept up the weathered steps, eased open the warped door, and entered the hallway. He found a room that overlooked the street. The place was littered with broken bottles, fallen curtains, and pack-rat droppings. He shoved an iron bed frame away from the window and looked through the streaked, wavy glass. From this vantage, he had a good view of the saloon where the mules stood. It wouldn't be a long vigil because of Boyd's need for water, Charvein thought. He was still thirsty himself, although he'd drunk the barley coffee and taken a parting swig from Sandoval's canteen.

He leaned his rifle against the wall and knelt by the window. He sorely missed a pair of field glasses to get a closer view of the saloon, although he doubted he'd learn any more unless he were close enough to see inside.

The hours of the morning dragged, and Charvein caught himself dozing in the heat, head in hands, as he sat crosslegged on the floor beside the window.

The braying of a mule jolted him. One of the mules no doubt voicing his protest at having nothing to drink.

Charvein peeked out the streaked window. The mules weren't braying for water—they were welcoming company. Three horsemen slowly approached from the far end of the street. They reined up at the saloon. Boyd appeared at the door, pistol in hand. There was a quick, heated exchange, but Charvein couldn't hear the words.

Two men on horseback raised their hands to show they intended no harm. Boyd let them dismount. The larger of the two dragged off the third rider, whose hands were tied in front of him—or rather, her. Her long dress was ripped up the center to facilitate riding astride. The big man shoved her aside. She stumbled and her straw hat slipped off, allowing shoulder-length hair to fall across her face. The two men paid her no attention.

Boyd kept them covered while they talked. The big man took off his hat and wiped a sleeve across his face. Charvein recognized him: Martin Stepenaw, a slow-witted, brutal giant reputed to be impervious to pain. The smaller

man, then, must be Glen Savage, dubbed "the Weasel" by
the newspapers.

"All hail! The gang is back together," Charvein breathed,
surveying the reunion. Had the governor been bribed into
releasing these two as well, knowing they'd follow their
leader to the gold? Doubtful. It appeared they'd coerced a
woman to accompany them.

Charvein felt confident he could deal with one man—
even one as dangerous as Boyd—as long as the ex-convict
didn't know anyone else was in town. But now there were
three, and the woman was an added complication. Charvein
took a deep breath. He'd have to be extra cautious and somehow get closer to find out what they were talking about.

Just then, Boyd motioned for them to come inside. Stepenaw grabbed the woman by the arm and yanked her with
him as they entered.

Charvein gripped his rifle and crept out of the room and
down the outside stairway. Having made sure they weren't
in sight, he darted across Center Street and between two
buildings. The growing heat of the sun was causing the
breeze to stir. A tumbleweed bounced along the street to
where it finally joined several others banked against the
wall of a shed.

Charvein moved toward the rear of the saloon, sliding
along behind the buildings, then squeezed into a four-foot-
wide space between the saloon and an empty store. There
were no windows in this side of the saloon, but the weathered boards had warped and shrunk, opening a crack where
he could listen to what was said. He squatted beside a rain
barrel and put an eye to the crack. He could see only partial
figures moving.

"Gimme one o' them sarsaparillas you're drinking," a
voice demanded.

"You boys ain't gonna offer the lady a drink first?" Boyd's mocking voice said.

"Just gimme one o' them damned bottles," Stepenaw rumbled.

After a moment of silence he said, "That's some better. But it didn't hardly knock the edge off my thirst."

"That's all you get for now," said Boyd.

Although Charvein could barely see movement inside, he suspected Boyd was backing up his statement with the point of a gun. "Didn't you boys bring any water?"

"Some," another, higher voice said. The Weasel was speaking. "But we come away in one helluva hurry. Just had time to scoop three water bags full from a horse trough."

"You had time to pick up this woman," Boyd said.

"It ain't what you're thinkin'," Savage said. "If we hadn't snatched her outta the warden's office, we never woulda got outside those walls alive. Kept the guards from gunnin' us down."

"So, what are you going to do with her now?" Boyd asked.

"Hang on to her for a while. She might be our insurance yet."

"You sayin' you and Marty will use her for a hostage because you led a posse right to this town?"

"Ain't no posse coulda followed us through that windstorm last night. *I* couldn't have followed us, and *I* knew where we were headed. We damned near lost our way as it was. Naw, our trail was wiped clean by the blowing dust."

"So let me get this straight," Boyd said. "Three horses and three people survived on three bags of water all the way out here?"

"We found us a little tank cupped in hollow rock in one o' them canyons back yonder or we woulda died. Scummy water. About dried up. Just enough to keep the horses going. But if we don't get these horses water soon, they're gonna die and we'll be stranded in this town."

Several moments of silence followed.

"Let's split up that gold, then look for water in these here mountains," Stepenaw said in a deep, raspy voice. "All this palavering is making my throat drier and wasting time."

"There's no gold to split up," Boyd said.

"We ain't got time for no damned jokes," Weasel said.

"I already looked where we hid it and it's not there."

In the silence, Charvein could hear floorboards creaking as the men shifted and moved.

"Then where do you think it is?" Savage asked.

"Beats me. Somebody musta took it while we were in prison."

"We hid it good."

"I know, but it's not there now," Boyd insisted.

"You think some animal drug it off?"

"Gold ingots don't smell like food. What animal would mess with them? The shiny color might've attracted some kind of birds, but it woulda taken a condor or eagle to lift a two-pound ingot."

"Pack rats, maybe? They're probably all around this place."

"There were sixty of those bars, and they were in twelve canvas sacks, five ingots to a sack, each sack weighing ten pounds. Weren't no evidence of the sacks or the gold. You telling me some critter, or even a pack of critters, made off with them?" Boyd said, derisively. "I been to the Yukon and seen wolverines strong enough to do it, but there ain't no wolverines here. I searched for a sign of any kind, but it was like nothing had ever been there."

Charvein heard Martin Stepenaw clump across the floor and out the front door, followed by the other two. Marc's legs were cramping in his squatting position so he stood up and stepped silently along the wall toward the front of the building, watching where he placed each foot to avoid the empty bottles and trash in the narrow passage. He reached the corner and crouched, removing his hat, then slid one eye around the corner. The big man laid his hand on one of the folded canvas bags on Boyd's pack mule. Boyd was watching him, curiously, but had holstered his own Colt.

"These the sacks you were gonna haul it in?" Stepenaw asked.

"Yeah," Boyd said.

Charvein withdrew and listened.

"I don't believe you needed these sacks," Stepenaw's slow, raspy voice said. "I got a strong hunch them old sacks was still good and you got the gold and stashed it away someplace before we got here."

"Why in hell would I do that?" Boyd asked. "I didn't even know you were coming." He sounded frustrated. "I just got here a few hours ago myself."

Sudden scuffling and grunting—the sounds of a fight. "What the hell you doing?" Boyd yelled.

Charvein gripped his rifle and risked a peek. The big man had Boyd's arms pinned in a bear hug. "Git his gun!" he rasped to Weasel.

Glen Savage snatched the Colt from Boyd's holster.

Charvein's heart was beating faster as he pulled back and crouched down.

Boots scuffed and clumped across the boardwalk, and there were sounds of heavy breathing. "Get him inside and tie him to that post!" Stepenaw said. "Then we'll git the truth out of him."

FOUR

"Roust yourselves outta there, you lazy bastards!"

Buck Rankin, former deputy U.S. marshal, shoved each of the four blanket-humped figures with his boot toe.

One of the men sat up and squinted at him in the gray light. "What's the big rush, Buck? We'll catch up." He raked his fingers through disheveled hair, an untamed rooster tail springing up. "Storm likely got them like it got us."

The other three stirred, coughing and spitting as they crawled, fully clothed, from under the protective blankets, shaking off a coating of dust.

"Damned good thing there's a reward for those two," one of the men mumbled.

"Hope it's worth it," another said.

"A thousand per man. How long would it take you coffee coolers to earn that kind o' money?" Rankin said. "Scrounge up some brush and get a fire going for breakfast. And hustle it up. I want to be in the saddle by sunup."

Rankin turned his back and walked away from the group so they wouldn't see the frustration on his stubble-covered face. He stretched his sore leg but made sure he exhibited no limp. He and his makeshift posse of volunteers had gotten a quick jump on pursuing prison escapees Stepenaw and Savage and their female hostage. He'd hoped to overtake and capture them before they could get a long head start. But Mother Nature had stepped in to stop the chase by buffeting them with a furious dust and sand storm. They were caught in the open and became disoriented. Forced to dismount, they'd huddled under their blankets and covered their horses' heads from the stinging blast that howled through the night.

The men behind him grumbled about lack of sleep as they untied two big coffeepots from the saddles and rattled around in their saddlebags for tin cups and bacon.

Buck admitted to himself that it didn't really matter if they were on the trail by sunup or a little later. Their advantage was gone; and worse, he had no idea what direction their quarry had taken, since all tracks on the soft crust of the playa had been swept away. There was a good chance the two convicts and their hostage were bogged down somewhere by the storm. But now pursuit would settle into a dogged chase, and he didn't relish that since he had to drag along these soft amateurs as his posse.

Only one member of his posse deserved respect—Schooner Douglas—a saloonkeeper and as hard a man as Rankin had ever encountered. But Douglas was addicted to drink and couldn't be trusted long enough to get the job done right.

The other problem was more personal. Rankin rubbed the bulging muscle behind his right thigh, stiff and sore from long hours in the saddle. Four years ago a bullet had ripped through his hamstring. The wound had not healed properly, causing much pain when he tried to run or climb or otherwise put pressure on the leg, but mostly when he had to sit a saddle for long stretches. He suspected his superiors in the U.S. Marshal Service had used not only the wound but also his age—fifty—as an excuse to force him into retirement. Since then, he'd survived on odd jobs to supplement his meager pension. That was the reason he was here now. The sheriff in Carson City had needed someone with experience to pursue the two men who'd overpowered a guard and taken a woman hostage to force their way out of state prison. They'd stolen guns, horses, and even taken the precaution of loading up with three water bags before riding east into the desert.

The sheriff, who was involved in a court case, quickly hired Buck to recruit a posse and give chase. Rankin was more than happy to have the job, especially since he'd be in line for a sizable reward put up by the state and by the wealthy brother of the woman being held hostage.

Inhaling a deep lungful of the fresh morning air, Rankin could hardly believe it had ever been clouded with dust. Why in hell did he put up with this harsh country? He should've gone back years ago to the more temperate climate of Missouri. But the bitterness and hatred surrounding the Civil War had driven him to seek a fresh start in Nevada—and he'd just stayed.

Even without a reward, he would draw his pay for the time spent on the chase. He wondered briefly if he should just abandon the pursuit and return to Carson, saying they'd lost the trio in the storm. Then he could shed these other men and start out again on his own. If successful, he would not have to share the reward. But that would mean publicly admitting defeat, not to mention four more days of extra riding back and forth.

If there was one thing his late mother had taught him, it was to never look back. Whatever happens, keep going ahead, she'd urged him. Do your best, and don't be afraid to take chances. He would keep going for now. These convicts, after spending four years in lockup with little opportunity for exercise, wouldn't be hardened to the trail. They'd be susceptible to heat, dust, and hardships. Buck smiled grimly to himself. He was tougher than they were, and he aimed to prove it. Water was the main problem. It was very heavy to carry, sloshing around, and easily lost through accidental spills or punctures of the full leather skins slung across their packhorse. They likely had enough to last another day, allowing the minimum for their horses to survive. No water for washing—only for drinking—until they could find more. Normally a fastidious man, Rankin had long ago discovered that going dirty and unshaven for days on end was the worst part of this work.

His immediate problem was what direction to take from here. The inexperienced men boiling the coffee would look to him for leadership. They were a long way out on this trackless dry lake bed, with low mountain ranges spiking up in the distance. Would the convicts have headed for the shelter of the mountains when the storm blew up, and would they have been able to reach them? Rankin had a general map of the region in his head. To supplement that, he had two tools at his disposal—a pair of field glasses and a pocket compass.

He reached into his shirt pocket and extracted a pair of wire-rimmed spectacles with smoked lenses. As far as his posse knew, they were for protection from sunlight. In actuality, they were prescription lenses.

Uncasing the field glasses, he brought them to his eyes, adjusted the focus for distance, and carefully scanned the playa. But he was forced to remove the spectacles to get the eyepieces close enough to his head for a good view.

If the escapees had been caught out by the storm, there was no sign of them now—only foreshortened distances of

nothing. It was growing lighter by the minute as the edge
of the sun peeked over the horizon. Rising heat waves had
yet to distort detail of the mountains. Only a few scrub
mesquite bushes clung tenaciously to the parched soil. No
other vegetation, no animals, no men—a dead planet as far
as he was able to see. He lowered the glasses. He'd have to
rely on his hunches, based on experience.

His leg began to ache, so he dropped to one knee to ease
the pain. It must not distract from his mental calculations.
As near as he could recall, the convicts and their hostage had a three-hour head start. Figure four, to be safe.
The armed breakout had occurred during the noon meal
at the prison. According to eyewitnesses, they jumped a
guard, took his gun, and shot their way into the warden's
office, where they captured a woman clerk for a hostage.
Using her as a shield, they forced the guards to open the
gate. From there, the escapees stole three saddled horses
tied in front of a hardware store, then relieved the store
owner of several coated canvas bags and filled them from
the watering trough in front. Forcing their woman hostage
onto the third horse, they galloped straight east out of Carson, making for the vast, open desert.

Buck tried to put himself in the place of the convicts. In
the rush to get away, he would have galloped for a couple
of miles before slowing the winded horses. Then what? As
the adrenaline ebbed, and they realized they were safe for
the time, they probably walked their mounts for a couple of
hours while watching their back trail for pursuit. This as-
sumption was confirmed by the very obvious hoofprints the
posse picked up in the soft crust at the edge of the vast
playa. How far would they have traveled before the storm
caught them in late afternoon?

A minimum of twenty miles, maximum of thirty, he
figured. The trail led in a straight line due east. Blowing

dust and darkness had finally shut down pursuit. This morning, the trail was obliterated. The convicts' head start should put them roughly eighteen miles ahead, Buck estimated—over the horizon and out of sight, even on a completely flat, featureless plain where fifteen miles would be the normal visual distance of a man on horseback. But, would they continue in a straight line, knowing they were leaving a trail obvious to a blind man? Yes, they would, assuming they wanted to put as much distance between themselves and Carson as possible. Now nature had come to their rescue by erasing their back trail.

If anyone happened to catch up to them, the fugitives still had a woman hostage as a last resort. At nightfall, when they wanted to camp, they'd look for the hidden shelter of a mountain canyon. Rankin figured the night wind fiercely blowing the dust had caught them in the open before they could reach the mountains, just as it had the posse. He decided, lacking any evidence of a direction change by their quarry, to continue heading due east.

What about the woman hostage? He knew her only by sight. She was young and slim and did clerical work in the warden's office. He assumed she'd be able to keep up and endure whatever these convicts could endure, provided they didn't mistreat her.

The smell of coffee brought him back to the present, and Buck rose from his kneeling position and turned back to the small campfire. Bacon was beginning to sizzle in the frying pan.

Late that afternoon, Buck held up his hand to halt his slow-moving posse. He uncased his field glasses and focused on something a few hundred yards ahead. It wasn't a rock or a plant, but neither was it moving.

While they were halted, he dismounted to ease the stiff-ness in his leg. He would lead his tired horse for a time. The other four did the same.

When they finally got close, Buck recognized the dust-covered carcass of a horse or mule. Shreds of hairy hide remained, but scavengers had done a thorough job of strip-ping the body of anything edible. Even the disarticulated bones had been gnawed, probably by night-roaming coyotes or wolves from the nearby mountains. This animal hadn't been dead more than a couple of days, Rankin estimated, walking around it and nudging the skull with his toe. Flies and maggots were still working. He squatted by the skeleton to take a closer look. A bullet hole in the temple? Of course. It figured. The rider had shot his horse rather than have it die of thirst. A saddle that lay nearby might provide a clue. But it contained no name or initials, and any saddlebags were missing. There was nothing unique about the saddle that might tell something of its ownership. It was well worn and could even have belonged to a livery.

He straightened up and looked around. The kill was too old to be one of the mounts that had carried the escapees. Somebody else was out here on this lonely playa, appar-ently in dire straits as well. Only a few tracks—wolf or coyote—were evident, made since the wind had erased all other traces.

"Water the horses while we're stopped," he directed.

The men poured their hats full of the precious liquid from the skin pouches. This had the added benefit after-ward of cooling their heads with the wet felt.

When they were done, Buck swung into the saddle and motioned them forward. He didn't need his compass to ride directly away from the westering sun. He had no idea if they were on the trail of the escapees or not, but he never let on to his men; better to keep them thinking he had the observation and tracking instincts of an Apache. Or maybe they were too tired to even care what he was doing, since they hadn't spoken for the last two hours. In truth, he was able to detect, now and then, an indentation that looked unnatural, out of place. Several times, he reined up, dismounted, and went down on hands and knees to examine what could have been a dust-filled hoofprint. The last time he did this, he struggled to his feet hoping his men would mistake a sober mien for a wise and thoughtful attitude. In reality, he wondered if he'd just taken a very close look at a natural hollow scooped out by the erratic wind then filled by blowing dust. He climbed back into the saddle, aching leg weighing a hundred pounds, and continued as if oblivious to the curious looks of his posse.

The sun made a silent, fiery exit below the distant mountains. Almost immediately, the air began to cool. With the drop in temperature, a slight breeze began to blow, the heavier, cooler air from the mountains sliding downslope to replace the superheated air in the wide, dead valley. The gentle breeze felt pleasantly cool at first. Then, it began to increase, until it was picking up dust and stinging grit. By the time dusk had faded into complete darkness, no stars were visible. The air above and all around them was filled again with blowing dust.

Buck pulled up his bandanna to cover his mouth and nose, tugged down his hat brim, and hunched forward in the saddle, determined to ride it out for several more hours to make up for lost time.

He hadn't counted on his four men whining and complaining they were tired, hungry, and thirsty and wanted to camp.

"Wait until we get across the playa into the shelter of the

mountains," Buck growled at them, raising his voice to be heard above the increasing gusts.

But within the hour, even he had to admit defeat in the face of another nightly onslaught. They pulled up in the middle of God-knew-where and made another camp with no fire, watered their horses, took a long drink themselves, pulled off their saddles and blankets, and made as good a shelter as possible. The horses stood with heads drooping, rumps toward the buffeting wind. The men had to wipe the dirt from the animals' nostrils with damp rags. Then they put handfuls of grain into nosebags and strapped them on so the bags would help filter the blowing dust.

Even Buck suffered the long, miserable night with only brief snatches of sleep while the endless hours of windy darkness ground away at their endurance.

FIVE

Is there no honor among thieves? Charvein wondered. *Apparently not among these thieves.* He'd been listening to Stepenaw and Weasel applying aggravating discomforts, mixed with outright torture, to Denson Boyd for more than a half hour. Boyd howled and cursed them, while he continued to deny any knowledge of the cached gold.

Charvein decided it was time to slip away. He'd heard and seen enough for now. It didn't matter to him what these escapees did to Boyd. Marc's job was to find out where the gold was hidden. To that end, all he had to do was lie low, wait, and watch. He rose from a crouch on stiffened legs and started to move away. His foot was asleep, and he kicked a rusty can that clattered against some empty bottles. To his ears, the noise was deafening. He froze.

Sudden silence inside the saloon. "What the hell was that?" Stepenaw said.

"Ah, just the wind blowing trash around outside," Weasel answered.

"Ow! You bastard! You're breaking my finger!" Boyd

yelled. "I tell you I don't know where the gold is. I can't tell you what I don't know. Ahh! I get loose from here, I'll break your damn head!"

Charvein, holding his breath, tried again to turn without making any noise in the tight space between the buildings. The butt of his rifle scraped the wooden wall of the saloon.

"Dammit, there's sumpin' out there, I tell ya!" Stepenaw said. "I'm gonna look."

"You're hearing ghosts," the Weasel said.

"Ghosts don't bang on walls and rattle tin."

Charvein took advantage of a sudden gust of wind to limp toward the alleyway, circulation beginning to return to his tingling foot.

Just as he emerged from between the buildings, the back door of the saloon opened. The wind caught and slammed it, crashing, back against the building.

Charvein's heart skipped a beat, and he jumped inside a shed that looked to be a combination tool shed and stable.

Stepenaw thrust his head out the back door and looked up and down the alley. Then he stepped out and, gun in hand, walked toward Charvein's hiding place, poking his head into the outhouse, then into the open back door of the mercantile. The wind gusted, blowing dust and rolling tin cans from a trash pile. Stepenaw shielded his face against the flying grit but continued his search, glancing in the back doorways of vacant buildings. The next building was the shed. Charvein held his breath, clutching his rifle. There was no back door or window for escape.

Stepenaw yanked open the sagging door and thrust his head inside the shadowed interior. Charvein, standing to one side, slammed the butt of his rifle against the big man's head. Stepenaw fell like a thick tree. Charvein looked out but saw no one. He leapt over the fallen man, sprinted across the alley, and ducked between two buildings. Running around to Center Street in front, he paused to catch his breath and let his heart rate slow.

Charvein moved back toward the saloon, hoping he hadn't given himself away. The gusting wind, banging a shutter and rattling a tin shed, covered any noise he made. But it was daylight, and he had to remain out of sight. Crouching by the edge of the porch, he watched the saloon. In less than five minutes, Stepenaw staggered out into the main street from between the buildings, a hand to his temple.

"Savage!" he cried. The stiff wind whisked away his words. "*WEASEL!*" he roared, then flinched at the effort, gripping his head with both hands as he stumbled up onto the wooden walk in front of the saloon.

Weasel came out the door. "What the hell's wrong with you?"

"Somebody hit me."

"Who?"

"I didn't see him."

"Probably a ghost."

"You think a ghost did this?" He pointed at the gash on the side of his head. "Look at that knot!"

"You likely fell and hit your head."

"You calling me a liar?"

"No, no. But you could be mistaken. We're alone in this town. Maybe you tripped and banged your head on something and just thought somebody hit you. You're just stunned and don't remember things real clear." Savage, in spite of his assurances, glanced up and down the street.

"Somebody clubbed me, I tell you! We're not alone here."

"Okay, okay. Come on inside and let me take a gander at it. We'll leave off working on Boyd for now and go have a look around, but it's a waste of time. There's nobody else here—unless it's something that ain't human."

"You keep laughing at me, I'll smash you into a grease spot."

"I ain't laughing at you," Weasel said fawningly. "But remember, if it weren't for me planning the breakout, you wouldn't even be here now."

"Yeah," the big man replied, gingerly touching his bruised head with his fingertips, "but if it weren't for me, you wouldn't have thought of taking that woman hostage. That's the only reason we got out of Carson City alive."

"You're right. Let me have a look at that gash. Your head's so damned hard, nothing short of a boulder could hurt it."

The two men disappeared into the saloon.

Charvein caught his breath. He felt relieved Weasel didn't believe anyone was in Lodestar. He waited a few moments, then cautiously crept away. Staying in the shelter of the buildings, he loped back toward the tunnel where he'd left Sandoval. He slid behind the brush concealing the entrance to the tunnel. The burro and the mule were there, but Sandoval was not. Charvein stepped toward the opening where the tunnel extended into the mountain. Hearing a noise, he flattened himself against the wall. Sandoval emerged from the tunnel carrying several canteens of water slung on straps from his shoulders.

Charvein relaxed. "What's this? Going on a trip?"

"No, señor. I am only bringing the daily supply of water for us and the animals." He set the half dozen canteens on the stone-and-dirt floor. "Would you like me to show you where the water is, in case you need to get some yourself?"

"Yes." Charvein wondered why the man hadn't carried a light into the dark tunnel.

"This way," Sandoval said, handing Charvein three large canteens and picking up two empty metal buckets as well.

They had walked in blackness for at least a hundred paces when a faint spot of light appeared in the distance. As they approached, Charvein began to make out an indirect light shining down a vertical shaft from above.

Sandoval stopped, and Charvein moved up beside him and peered down. Three feet below where they stood was a shiny, unruffled surface.

"Clean water," Sandoval said. "No quicksilver, no dead animals, no dirt except what might blow down from above in a hard dust storm."

Charvein wondered how Sandoval knew this for certain. "Do the other shafts have clean water, too?"

"Some do, but it is down deep. The top of this shaft is not at the crest of the mountain like the others are. The water in those other shafts would be difficult to reach because all the lifts are broken or rusted. Those men out there—if they even knew water was down here—would need many ropes tied together to reach it." He smiled in the dim light. "And I have taken most the buckets to use myself."

Sandoval put the canteens in a net and tied it closed at the top with a cord. Charvein noted a two-pound chunk of iron in the net to make it sink. The Mexican lowered the net into the water by the slender rope. Air bubbles roiled the surface as it sank and the canteens filled. An ingenious way to fill several containers with narrow necks in a hurry, Charvein thought.

When the bubbles stopped, the two men hauled up the net with its cargo of fresh water and capped the canteens.

"Why don't you use a torch or lantern in here?" Charvein asked as they felt their way back in the dark.

"I need both hands to carry this," he replied. "I know this tunnel. Long ago, I ran out the rats. Besides, a light would only alert anyone who might be looking down the shaft, or a stranger waiting to ambush me in my cave."

Sandoval seemed to have thought of every contingency. But then, what else did he have to do but think? His answer had been cautious but not fearful. Yet, given the fact that Charvein and four other strangers had found their way to this deserted town, maybe Sandoval had good reason to be careful. Except for an occasional trip to town, he was entirely on his own here.

While Sandoval watered his animals, Charvein related what had happened. "I'll leave them alone for a short time until they decide to make a move," Charvein concluded, thinking aloud.

"*Bueno*," Sandoval said. "So now, let us eat. There are beans left from last night. It would not be wise to make a fire while they are here."

Charvein nodded. "I can't stay here long. I must keep them in sight from a distance."

Sandoval dug out the food.

Around a mouthful of beans a few minutes later, Charvein said, "Why do you stay here alone with your animals?"

"Because I find them better company than most of my own kind," he replied.

Charvein took this as a mild rebuff to mind his own business, so he let the subject drop. He finished his meager meal in silence. Then he sat down on the floor and pulled off his boots. His wrinkled white feet appeared to have been boiled. Broken blisters stung. "You got any socks I can buy?" he asked.

"No, señor. But these might fit you." He went to a box along the wall, opened it, and rummaged inside. Returning, he tossed over a pair of moccasins. Charvein ran his hand over soft doeskin of the thigh-high footgear. The soles were made of tough, thick rawhide. "Apache *n'deh b'keh*. How did you come by these?"

"I have not always lived in Lodestar," Sandoval said.

Charvein tugged the moccasins on and stood up, then turned down the tops, tying them just below his knees. He immediately reveled in the comfort. "Don't need any socks with these. How much?"

Sandoval frowned. "This is not a store, señor. Those are a gift from me to you."

"In addition to saving my life and giving me food and water, you are taking care to be sure my feet are not ruined," Charvein marveled.

"The best kind of footgear for the desert."

A strange man, but generous. "You did not make these yourself?"

"Those required the skill and patience of a Mimbreno squaw."

"Thanks. These feel much better than those worn-out boots." He walked a few steps. "They make no noise, and they're light and comfortable." He picked up a full canteen and took a long drink. He hoped Sandoval was right about this cold water not containing any dangerous chemicals. It didn't even taste of rust, as he had half expected. "Mind if I take this with me?"

Sandoval gestured at the haul they'd just made. "There is plenty more."

Charvein turned to leave, then came back and propped his rifle against the wall. "I have my six-gun and knife, if I need them. Less weight to carry."

"When will you return?"

"By dark, or sooner, depending on what they do." He hesitated, not wanting to sound as if he were giving orders to his benefactor. "We are downwind of those men and their horses and mules, so your animals will catch their scent."

"I will keep them quiet. *Vaya.*"

Charvein slipped outside, peeked through the thick brush to be sure he was in the clear, then turned away from town and skirted the bulge of the hill before he began to ascend the steeper side of the mountain, toward the hoisting works at the summit. If these men couldn't find the gold, their next move, obviously, would be to search for water.

The climb was steeper and more difficult than he'd expected. He was glad he'd elected to leave his rifle behind, since he had to use both hands to grasp low-growing mesquite and sage to help pull himself up, his moccasins slipping in the loose, rocky soil, the full canteen banging against his side. Twice he paused for breath before reaching the top.

Crawling the last few yards over the lip of the summit, he spotted the derelict tin sheds housing the hoisting works of four mines, stretching along the spiny crest of the mountain range. Apparently, rich veins of ore had been discovered below the unpromising Nevada mountain.

He got to his feet. The prevailing west wind brought the sound of voices. How close? He had only enough time to scrabble back and flatten himself in a thick patch of mesquite before Stepenaw and Savage trudged over the crest about thirty yards away. They had come up a more gradual slope and didn't have to crawl. Nevertheless, they were puffing and blowing from their climb and failed to look in his direction.

"We'll cut you loose," Weasel said to Boyd who was being led by a loop of rope around his neck, "if you promise not to give us any trouble."

Boyd's hands were still tied in front of him.

"How the hell can I give you trouble?" Boyd snarled. "You got my guns." He took a deep breath. "Okay, I promise."

Weasel untied Boyd's hands. With obvious relief, Boyd then slid the loop off over his head.

"You ain't holding no grudges, now, are ya? After what the big man done?" Weasel asked.

"Anything I got against you boys, we can settle later,"

Boyd said, rubbing his wrists. "Right now, we're all in the same fix. If we don't find water pretty quick, we'll be leaving our bones in Lodestar." He wiped a sleeve across his mouth, then spat. "Nothing but cotton," he said.

Charvein, lying concealed by the thick patch of mesquite, wondered where their female hostage was. He pictured her still trussed up in the saloon below. He wondered if they'd given her even a taste of sarsaparilla to wet her mouth. She had to be as thirsty as they were.

"Let's get to lookin' down these shafts," Weasel said.

"Yeah," Boyd said. "I'd forgot till an hour ago these mines flooded when they dug to groundwater. Put 'em outta business and made Lodestar a ghost town within a year."

"The water must still be down there, like in a well," Stepenaw said. "Don't reckon it's drained off anywhere." A makeshift bandage was wrapped around the big man's head under his hat.

Charvein recalled how hard he'd popped that head with the butt of his rifle and wondered that Stepenaw was still walking around.

"Well, Mother Nature mighta sucked it back up 'tween the rocks."

"Crap!" Stepenaw said. "Let's go look."

They trooped toward the nearest tin shed. Rusted machinery showed through where a couple of the tin sides had blown off.

Charvein noted that the two escapees were armed with handguns, but they had not hauled Boyd's big Sharps up the steep hill. If it came to a fight, it would be his one Colt and the element of surprise against their handguns and sense of desperation.

Even after the men were inside what was left of the tin shed, they were still within sight, and Charvein couldn't creep away without being noticed. He could hear them talk-

ing and caught a word here and there as they tried to see
down into the shaft.

". . . too dark," Stepenaw said.

"Try . . . chunk o' iron," Weasel said.

A few seconds of silence.

"Thought I heard a splash," Boyd said.

"How the hell we gonna get it? Must be two hundred feet
down."

They fell to discussing how long their lariats were if all
strung together.

Charvein was only half-listening as he cast about for a
way to escape unseen. Somehow, he had to distract their
attention. If they came back out of the shed, they'd walk
within twenty yards of where he lay. He looked around
on the rocky ground and selected a fist-size rock. The small
shed attached to the rear had probably served as the office
for the mine superintendent. While the three clustered at
the hoist near the shaft, their backs to him, he drew his legs
up under him in a crouch, then stood. Shrugging his shoulders, he limbered up his arm, wound up, and heaved the
rock in a high arc at the tiny adjoining tin shed nearly fifty
yards away.

SIX

Charvein flattened himself within the patch of mesquite a second before the rock clattered onto the sloping tin roof. It hit and bounced, rolling off the back with a thunderous racket.

Startled, the three men froze. Stepenaw and Savage whipped out their pistols.

Two seconds of silence. "What the hell was that?" Savage said.

"I told you we weren't alone here," Stepenaw said. "I told you."

"Shut up and listen," Weasel snapped.

Silence except for the wind.

Charvein held his breath.

"Reckon we better find out if that was some wild critter," Savage said, taking a step forward.

Stepenaw waved his gun at Boyd. "You first."

"Probably something blew off the top of this dilapidated shed," Boyd said calmly, taking the lead at gunpoint.

The three cautiously advanced on the closed door. Stepenaw held up a hand, and they paused. The big man kicked a booted heel against the dried wooden door. It slammed open into an attached rear office.

The instant it crashed inward off its frame, Charvein leapt to his feet and dashed toward the crest of the hill. He was downwind, and the outlaws' attention was focused away from him. Keeping an eye on the trio until the last second, he jumped over the edge out of sight, bounding nimbly down the steep slope, moccasin-clad feet bouncing from soft ground to rock as fast as his eyes could pick up the terrain below. Making no more noise than a mountain goat, he traversed the incline and reached the bottom in less than a minute.

Glancing back once, he sprinted toward the shelter of the nearest building at the lower end of Center Street, where he halted, panting, to be sure he hadn't been observed. Now that they knew water existed in the bottom of the shaft, they'd be busy devising a way to reach it. They'd fail to discover the source of the diverting noise, which would further baffle them. Hopefully, it would start another argument.

Breathing heavily, Charvein jogged up Center Street toward the Red Horse Saloon, keeping close to the buildings, the false fronts of which shielded him from sight of the hill behind. This might be his only chance to free the woman hostage. Cat-footing up onto the boardwalk, he carefully peered around the open doorway. At first, he saw no one and assumed they had relocated her. But then a movement across the room caught his eye. The woman lay on the floor at the end of the bar, bound hand and foot to the brass foot rail.

She was not gagged, and she opened her mouth as she saw him. But no sound issued from it. He must have been a sight, striding in, a sunburned wraith out of the sandy wastes of the Nevada desert, wild hair, a week of stubble on his lean cheeks, dirty clothes, gun and knife at his belt, wearing knee-high Apache moccasins.

He put a finger to his lips to signal quiet as he padded to her side and slipped out his belt knife to slice her ropes and free her.

"Water," she gasped, touching the canteen that still swung at his shoulder.

He slipped it loose and popped out the cork for her.

Trembling, she grasped it with both hands and began to drink, sloshing it down the front of her torn dress in her haste.

A few seconds later, she paused to get her breath, looking up at him with big eyes. Her white wrists and arms were scraped raw where she'd struggled against her ropes. She gulped down more water.

"Easy!" he said, taking the canteen gently, but firmly, from her. "Let that settle. There's plenty more."

"Thought I was going to die," she whispered hoarsely, licking her lips. "Never been so thirsty."

"Can you stand?" he asked quietly, reaching down to help her to her feet. She leaned weakly against the bar. "They would have killed me," she said, haltingly, as if learning to talk again after her mouth and throat were paralyzed.

"Maybe from neglect," Charvein said. "But not intentionally. You were their insurance."

She looked fearfully toward the door.

"You're right," Charvein said, interpreting her look. "Let's get out of here. They could be back any minute for their lariats."

"Why?"

"They found water at the bottom of a deep shaft and have to figure out a way to get at it. If you're still their prisoner, they might lower you down on one of those rusty cables with a water bag to bring it up for them." He took her by the elbow and guided her toward the back door. She stumbled and would have fallen had he not caught her around the waist.

"My foot's asleep," she explained.

He was glad it wasn't just general weakness; if worse came to worst, she'd have to be able to move quickly on her own.

He'd expected her to be full of questions about him, or where he'd come from, but such was not the case. It was almost as if she'd been expecting him—a dashing prince who was late for their rendezvous.

"Did they leave any weapons close by?" he asked.

She shook her head. "Don't think so."

"What about that long Sharps rifle Boyd had?"

She looked blank.

"Never mind. Let's go."

They went quickly into the alleyway, and he hurried her along toward the lower end of town, planning to leave her in Sandoval's care.

Suddenly he had another thought. "Wait right here," he said, thrusting her inside a handy privy.

"But I don't have to use this," she said, seemingly more lively as the water worked its restorative power.

"Just hide there a minute," he said, pushing the door shut.

He stopped to listen. But the sound he heard was the low whinny of a thirsty horse tied in front of the saloon. He hoped it was only thirst as he dashed back to the saloon. Good; no one in sight, but he had to hurry. He snatched up the fragments of rope he'd sliced from the woman's arms and legs. Let them wonder some more. The only evidence of his presence were a couple of distinguishable moccasin prints in a patch of undisturbed dust, and some dark spots of spilled canteen water on the dry boards. Let them think Indians were here—Indians with water. *That oughta set their teeth on edge.* He grinned.

". . . by God, you're on about that again . . ." The sound of Boyd's approaching voice startled him. He made for the back door quickly with the fragments of rope. Loping down the alley, he caught a glimpse of the three men trudging up the main street. Just as he'd thought, they were returning without trying to use the abandoned mine cable that lay strewn about on the summit.

He jerked open the privy door and grabbed the woman's arm, then tossed the pieces of cut rope down one of the long unused toilet holes.

They had to hurry now. There'd be an uproar when the men discovered her missing. Her circulation apparently restored, she had no trouble keeping up with him, even in her high-top shoes with the square, elevated heels. Her long dress was ripped up the middle to her waist, and more than a foot of material had been torn off the hem.

When they passed two more buildings, he pulled her to one side, and they dodged between Lawson's Mercantile and the Gold Nugget Assay office. He had to think one jump ahead of the outlaws. They'd probably come out the back door of the saloon. He didn't want to be in full view in the alley.

They held up, breathing hard, at the edge of the boardwalk on Center Street. The horses and mules still stood in front of the Red Horse Saloon, but there was no sign of the outlaws. Should they chance it in the street or on the boardwalk? If one of the men happened to step out front—Charvein swallowed—he and the girl would be easy targets. But they couldn't just wait here.

No sooner had the thought crossed his mind than he heard a shout and muffled cursing from the direction of the saloon. Time to go. It was now or never.

Before he could move, Stepenaw and Boyd burst out the front of the saloon and started down the middle of the street toward them. Boyd was arguing with the big man, who paid no attention.

"If you see her, don't shoot!" came a yell from Weasel in the alley. "We gotta take her alive. She ain't no good to us dead."

For some reason, they were making no effort to be quiet. Perhaps it was a ploy to make her panic and run out of hiding, like flushing quail. Why were they coming this direction? She could just as easily have escaped down the street the other way. No time to wonder about that. He and the girl had to hide—quickly. If only it were night. But it wasn't.

"Inside!" he whispered, shoving her ahead of him through the partially open door into the cluttered assay office. Where to hide? Behind the counter until the outlaws passed? No. If the trio decided to search the individual buildings, it would be all up with him unless he could somehow hold them off with his Colt. The men could easily see the scuff marks in the years of dust on the floor. He looked about quickly and stuck his head into the adjacent office behind the front counter. A desk, two chairs, a rotted curtain falling down from the window, papers scattered around on the floor—between the desk and the rear window, a faded red carpet covered an eight-foot-by-four-foot space of floor.

He sprang to the dirty window to scan the alley for the searchers, but caught his toe on the rug, nearly falling through the glass. Under the corner of the tacked rug his toe had jerked loose was an iron ring imbedded in the floor. He grabbed it and pulled. A heavy trapdoor, three feet by three came up on groaning hinges, further popping the tacks. Through the cobwebs, he could see only two or three steps leading down into the darkness.

He hesitated. Audible voices now, coming closer.

"Well, it's this or fight," Charvein said in a low voice.

She nodded, eyes big.

"Wait." He yanked the curtain down and used it to smudge out the dusty tracks in the outer office, backing into where they stood. They'd see a big spot of cleaner floor, but at least not the same tracks as in the saloon. He tossed the curtain into a corner. "Better you go first," he whispered, "so I can straighten this rug over the trapdoor. We shouldn't have to be down there more than a few minutes," he added, trying to allay her look of alarm.

Even if he'd left no tracks, there were obvious signs of the coating of dust being disturbed—evidence somebody had recently been here. With any luck, the three men wouldn't even come inside the assay office. He'd been lucky so far; maybe his luck would hold.

He handed her down the steps, then followed, pivoting the trapdoor on its hinges and easing it down as he reached around to pull the rug back into place over it. The tacks still held the rug at the other end, so it was no trouble to get it placed correctly.

Thump! He let the heavy door fall into place. Suffocating darkness closed over them.

SEVEN

He felt the woman clutching his arm tighter than necessary. They were standing at the bottom of the hole, only five steps from the top. The cellar—if that's what it was—was not more than six feet deep. Not even the tiniest sliver of light leaked through the solid floor. The air was stale. What was the purpose of this underground place—a fruit cellar, perhaps? No. Not beneath an assay office. Could be a secure and secret storage vault for valuable samples, in lieu of an office safe. What kind of town had this Lodestar been that the office required such a hiding place? He kept his mind busy to avoid thinking of the musty air, the spiders, cockroaches, and any other vermin down here with him.

The woman gasped and jumped, standing closer to him. "Something touched me."

"Sshhh!" He didn't know how long they should stay here. It was very possible the men would not even enter this building. He had no matches left to take a quick look at their surroundings, or to check his watch.

They waited . . . and waited . . . Time came to a halt. The

woman had no choice but to endure this as well, and she did so quietly, without complaint.

Just when he began to think eternity must have started, Charvein heard muffled voices and the thudding of boots on the floor above. He listened. The sounds came closer, boots clumping overhead, atop the rug on the trapdoor.

Charvein went up the three steps and pressed his ear to one of the planks above.

"Somebody's been here," Stepenaw said. "That Injun brought her here. Look, the dust is all scuffed around. Can't tell me spirits did that. They don't have no bodies."

Weasel's whiny voice piped up. "Spirits can do physical things, too. Ain't you never heard of doors slamming and drawers opening by themselves, and objects rising up in the air? Happens all the time in haunted houses. Spirits have control of our world, too."

The big man exploded. "Bullshit! Show me a ghost, and I'll believe you."

"Spirits don't have bodies. You can't see them. You can only see what they do."

"Ya know, to look at you, nobody'd think you're that damned stupid," Stepenaw said.

"Who're you calling stupid, you big pile o' mule dung?"

Charvein heard a clatter and the skittering of feet on the floor. Apparently, the big man was attacking the Weasel. "That's it. Go after each other," Charvein muttered. He heard nothing from Boyd, who was probably hoping the same thing.

A terrified yell. Sounded like Savage. Feet pounding. The sounds receded.

Charvein sighed. *They're gone.* But the next second he caught his breath. Footsteps inches from his ear. Boyd was walking around the room above. The steps paused, then moved. The smartest of the three must be inspecting the room and the partially wiped-out tracks in the dust. Boyd, the only one with sense, was figuring out that two sets of tracks came into the room, but none led out. Boyd was the one to be feared, yet he was probably still unarmed—the prisoner of the other latecomers.

Charvein eased his Colt out of its holster to be ready in case Boyd discovered the trapdoor. A scraping noise sounded just above, as if the rug were being scuffed aside with a boot.

This was not the time for confrontation. Let them think for a while longer they were dealing with actual ghosts in this ghost town. He stepped down and took the woman's arm. "Feel around and see if this room is any larger," he whispered in her ear. He swung his arm slowly, probing, feeling for the walls. On one side he encountered packed dirt. He could hear her bumping against something on the other side of him. He holstered his gun and ducked under the steps. His questing hands encountered nothing but cottony cobwebs. "This way," he whispered. If Boyd lifted the trapdoor and looked down, but didn't enter, they could flatten themselves against the wall under the steps or in a corner.

Charvein held the woman's hand and drew her after him, taking one tentative step after another into the blackness. Encountering no resistance and no wall, he moved a little faster, spurred on by the hollow sounds of someone fumbling with the ring in the trapdoor. He doubted Boyd, or either of the others—even if they weren't fighting in the street—was carrying more than a match to illuminate the underground passage. Four steps, five steps, ten . . . It was obviously a tunnel, but leading where? There was no smell *f* fresh air; in fact, the musty odor was becoming more *n*ounced, the air fouler.

ey went thirty paces, then the trapdoor's dry hinges

squealed. Charvein pushed the woman ahead of him and turned to walk backward, drawing his gun. Light shone down the steps, and Boyd's voice shouted something at the other men. "Hurry!" Charvein whispered. "If they come down the hole, we'll stop so they can't hear us."

The floor of the tunnel was level and fairly smooth. At intervals, Charvein's shoulder brushed an upright support post. He constantly raked cobwebs from his face. He was almost glad he could see nothing of their surroundings.

Loud, threatening voices came from behind them, and Charvein heard boots clumping on the board steps. The legs he could make out appeared to belong to Boyd, judging from the fancy, red-toed boots. No doubt the others had forced him to go down first and investigate.

Marc pulled the woman to a halt. They watched as Boyd took a few tentative steps into the darkness. Then a match flared in his hand. He held the tiny flame aloft and peered around. There was no way he could see beyond three or four feet.

Charvein held his breath. If they were using matches, it meant they had no torches, lanterns, or even candles. As he saw it, the men had two choices—they could give up the search and look for any stored coal oil, candles, or lanterns, or they could block the trapdoor and go on with their quest for water and gold. He much preferred the first choice. They knew the woman would not try to leave town on foot. As long as they guarded their mounts, they'd be reasonably sure she was still close by. They could afford to be patient about the hostage, but not about water. Every hour that passed meant the three men and their animals were becoming more and more desperate to reach the only source of water they'd discovered, at the bottom of the deep mine shaft.

He listened but couldn't make out the conversation be-

tween Boyd and the men above. Then Boyd retreated
through the trapdoor, and Weasel stepped down into the
hole, drew his Colt and fired three times in their direction. The muffled shots boomed like cannon fire, yellow
flame lancing from the muzzle. At the first shot, Charvein
grabbed the woman and threw her to the ground. The second ricocheted off the tunnel wall and clipped the top of his
ear. The third missed. Charvein swore fervently to himself,
though he couldn't hear his own muttering because of
being momentarily deafened by the blasts. He touched his
ear; his fingers came away wet and sticky.

"By God, if you're in there, woman, you'd best be haulin' your ass out here. Your only chance of survival is with
us. We ain't gonna kill you, but you'll die soon enough on
your own in this place." He paused. "We don't need you no
more since we got away safe. If some Injun's got you, you're
likely a lot worse off than you would be with us." A harsh
laugh followed, then he climbed up. The trapdoor thumped
closed, plunging them into darkness.

"You think they'll wait for me to come out?" she asked,
placing a hand on his shoulder.

"I think those shots were meant as a warning," Charvein
said, holding a dirty bandanna to his stinging ear. He had a
sudden urge to rush out and take them all on, but his judg-
ment told him this was neither the time nor the place for
that. His job was to locate the gold and report back to the
man who'd hired him. A simple enough assignment, but
one that was turning out to be a lot more complex than he'd
imagined.

"I doubt they really expect you to come out, even if
they're convinced you're down here," he replied. "Let's
wait thirty minutes to make sure they're gone, then try the
trapdoor. They might wait a few minutes, but then they'll

figure either one o' those random shots got you, or else you found another way out."

He knew he was taking a big chance. Even if he waited a half hour, he might push up the trapdoor into a hail of bullets. He hoped he was judging the short patience and long desperation of these three correctly. Boyd would have the most patience, but he was a virtual prisoner himself and would be forced to leave with the others. Besides, he had no stake in the welfare of this woman hostage; he was a man who looked out for his own interests.

Charvein waited a slow estimated half hour; in reality, it was probably fifteen minutes. The woman at his side did not utter a word the entire time.

"Okay," he finally said. "Let's give it a try."

He took her hand, and they retraced their steps. He counted their paces, but there was no way they could miss the spot, because he swung his arms in front of him and his hand bumped the steps.

"Stay here," he said, drawing his gun. Two steps up and he bent over and leaned the flat of his back into the door and pushed with his legs, exerting slow, upward pressure. The door did not budge. His heart sank, but he tried again, straining with all his strength. The door moved less than an inch.

He stepped back down to the floor and wiped a sleeve across his sweating brow. "They blocked it. Feels like something really heavy is holding it down."

"What do we do now?" she asked, her voice slightly shaky.

"Well, before we go any further, let's introduce ourselves. We haven't had time to formally meet. I'm Marc Charvein."

"Lucinda Barkley," she replied. "Just Lucy will do."

"Nice to know you, Lucy," he said, fumbling to take her hand.

"I . . . I want to thank you for rescuing me."

"Some rescue," he replied. "Took you right from the frying pan to the fire."

"You tried."

"For now, we're just two blind people who must rely on our other senses." He was stating the obvious, but he thought the sound of his voice would soothe her and talking would possibly give him time to think and formulate some plan of action. "Listen, Lucy, there must be something at the end of this tunnel. People don't dig tunnels that lead nowhere, unless they are in a mine."

"What if it's caved in?" she asked, her voice now calm, as if she were anticipating and accepting the worst.

He wished he could see her face to read her feelings.

"We'd gone nearly fifty yards before we came back. Let's go on until we find something—even if it's just a dead end."

She followed, holding on to his gunbelt as he led the way.

Breathing as shallowly as possible, he put the foul air out of his mind and focused on what might be ahead. But the total blackness was like a velvet glove smothering him. He hoped her thoughts were elsewhere.

The tunnel led on another seventy paces, although Charvein had lost exact count. He was walking with his Colt in hand, arm straight out and swinging slowly from side to side.

The barrel of his gun bumped something solid. He felt with his hand and encountered what seemed to be a door. This time they were certainly at the end. But why a door in a tunnel, unless it was to close off something on the other side?

"What is it?" she asked.

"A door, but not made of solid planks. Uhh! Got a handle, but it's rusted. Feels like an interior door with panels. Partly rotted. Move back a step. I'll try to bust through."

He aimed the thick sole of his right moccasin at the panel near the bottom. On the third kick with the ball of his foot, the panel splintered. Dim light filtered through. With renewed vigor, he thrust his shoulder at the upper portion and it splintered with little resistance. He kicked it down sufficiently for them to duck through. Dusty shafts of light sliced between the cracks in the floor overhead.

"Let there be light!" he intoned gratefully.

Six feet beyond, the tunnel ended in solid earth. After quickly piling larger pieces of the broken door atop one another, Marc stepped up but could barely touch the overhead boards. When his eyes got accustomed to the dim light, he saw that several steps had dried out and fallen in. They'd led up to another trapdoor.

Piling more debris of ruined stairs against one wall for support, he carefully climbed up, braced himself, and began to push. The overhead door gave, dirt sifting down into his face. He spat and snorted dusty air out his nose, then renewed his effort, shoving the door up several inches. A rush of sweet-smelling fresh air greeted him. "Lucy, come up here beside me. That's it . . . be careful. Now I'll boost you up on my shoulder while I brace us against the wall. You'll have to push up that trapdoor and wedge a few chunks of wood into the crack until I can shove you up through the hole. Then you can help me up."

Without question or complaint, she did as instructed. Within ten minutes, she climbed out and threw back the door, and then Charvein muscled his way up and over the lip.

"I think we're in the back room of a bank," Lucy said.

"Good as any," Charvein muttered. "If they decide to get a lantern and explore that tunnel, we'll be long gone. Be careful where you step in this dust. Let's see if we can muddle up any telltale signs for them, just in case."

Papers and ledger books lay scattered on the floor, among shards of broken glass and bird droppings.

"Walk on the balls of your feet out the front door," he said, gently setting the trapdoor back into place. Then he slid a filing cabinet over it. Pulling open one of the full drawers, he took out a sheaf of papers and scattered them over their tracks as he backed toward the front of the building. "That won't fool 'em long if they're serious about hunting us," he said, dusting off his hands.

The grimy front window was still intact, much of it covered by large peeling letters, painted in reverse on the inside of the glass.

He eased open the front door and looked back up the street. They were two blocks from the saloon—farther than he'd guessed. He suddenly felt uneasy when he realized the horses and mules were no longer standing out front. He looked down the street in the other direction. No sign of man or beast. As long as their mounts were visible, he had a fix on where the outlawas had set up headquarters. But now . . . "Maybe they took them to the old stable where I spent the night," he said aloud.

"What?"

"Their horses and mules."

"They'll have to water them soon or they'll die," she said. "They were in sad shape even before we got here."

He nodded.

"Can you spare another drink from your canteen?" she asked, licking her lips.

He handed her the canteen and she took a long drink. "I didn't leave you much," she said, shaking the container.

"I'm taking you where there's plenty more," he said.

"Come on." He grasped her hand. "I guess we'd better go out the back way. Safer than the main street."

They found a side office door leading into the alley. From there, they crept close to the backs of the buildings until they reached the edge of town. Charvein guided Lucy to Sandoval's screened hiding place, a quarter mile away along the base of the mountain. They brushed aside the thick bushes and entered. It was empty.

Sandoval stepped out from the mouth of the tunnel and eased down the hammer of his rifle. "We'll have to arrange a signal," he said. "This town is getting crowded."

"Good idea." Charvein made introductions and explained the situation.

"A hostage?"

"I don't think they care if I escape," she said, "now that they're not responsible for me. Besides, I'm stuck here, just like they are." Then her eyes fell on the burro and the mule at the far side of the cavern.

"Only as a last resort," Charvein said, noting her glance.

"You hungry?" Sandoval asked the woman. "When did you last eat?"

"Yesterday morning. No . . . the night before," she said. "But I was so thirsty, I wasn't hungry."

Sandoval nodded. "Sit down here and rest. I will prepare some food."

"Did you know about that tunnel between the assay office and the bank?" Charvein asked.

"Yes."

"I wanted to steal their animals," Charvein said. "But three horses and two mules were too many for me to handle at once. Besides, they might have brayed or whinnied and sounded the alarm. As it happened, I didn't have time, anyway. I was damned lucky to get her out before they came back." He sat down beside Lucy on the blanket. "These moccasins you gave me left tracks in the dust on the saloon floor."

Sandoval's serious face nearly relaxed into a grin. "So now they think there's an Indian in town."

"A ghostly Indian with water who made her ropes dissolve and disappear," Charvein added, throwing his head back with a hearty belly laugh that felt good. It had been too long.

"After dark, I'll risk a small fire just outside," Sandoval said. The thick brush will dissipate the little smoke."

"Not a good idea," Charvein said.

"Another strong southwest wind tonight," Sandoval said. "Thick with dust from the playa as it was the last two nights. They will never smell our tiny bit of smoke."

"Good," Charvein agreed. "As long as those men think we're ghosts and they don't have the water or gold, we're safe," he went on. "And . . . as long as they continue fighting among themselves. I hope they haven't given Boyd back his long Sharps." He stepped toward the entrance to the cavern. "Do those westerlies blow often, or in a certain pattern?"

Sandoval nodded. "I usually know when they will come. Tonight the wind will be strong enough to toll the bell in the San Juan tower, just as you heard it."

"Maybe I can work on their imaginations some more."

"The Paiute spirits will howl. They can be heard for a mile or more."

"Even better," Charvein grinned. "But these men have been here before—when they hid the gold someplace nearby. If they were here when the wind was strong, they'll know that sound for what it is."

They were interrupted by a squeal that rose piercingly on the breeze and then died. A chill went up Charvein's back, and his hand dropped to his Colt.

The look on Sandoval's face showed he was just as startled.

Then it came again—a long, wavering screech, fading into silence.

"Catamounts in these hills?" Charvein asked.

"I have never seen one, señor—unless they've been drawn here by the scent of game—horses and mules." His eyes were wide in the dark, somber face. "But what we just heard is not the scream of a wild creature—or anything else I've ever heard in my years upon this earth."

EIGHT

Charvein swallowed hard and struggled to get a grip on his emotions. There had to be an explanation for the sound. "I'll check it out," he said, snatching his Colt Lightning pump from where it leaned against the wall. "This time I'll take more firepower." He checked to make sure the magazine was full. "If I'm not back by daylight, come looking."

"Daylight?" Lucy said. "It's still two hours till dark."

"I plan to be back well before the west wind begins to howl. Oh, one more thing . . ." He selected a full canteen from the several full containers on the floor. "Save me a bite of supper." He grinned, then faded into the bosque that screened the entrance. He paused outside, waiting for the sound to come again. It did—this time a longer, more drawn out shriek than before. Somehow, it didn't strike Charvein as a natural sound. Possibly two mountain lions fighting? Hunting cats were silent. A couple of short squeals, and he got closer to figuring the direction—somewhere above and to the west of where he stood. Would he have to scale that mountain again?

Then the sound stopped. He skirted the base of the mountain, searching for a less severe incline. Ten minutes later, he discovered a wagon road that wound in a gradual ascent. He followed the overgrown, rutted road. The chilling feline squalling had stopped. If it was a large cat, it had apparently moved on.

The sun's rays slanted long across the parched earth. A warm, westerly breeze washed over him. He labored up the wagon road, his thighs burning from exertion. The wind dried his sweaty shirt and brow.

He paused for breath near the summit. The headframes of two mines came into view. The nearest one suddenly produced the nerve-chilling shriek. Charvein's heart jumped, and he dove to the ground, rifle at the ready. The noise died, then came again in two short bursts. He listened. It sounded mechanical. Seeing nothing, he climbed to his feet and crept forward, staying out of sight behind a huge pile of spoil. Fifty yards away stood the tin-sided building he'd seen earlier. Through gaps in the ruined structure, he saw the three outlaws working. The breeze brought indistinct voices. Their horses and mules were picketed nearby.

Then he saw the source of the screeching noise—a rusty pulley through which the men had rigged a thin cable. The greaseless sheave squalled in protest when forced to work after years of idleness. Evidently, they'd managed to find empty buckets and enough cable to reach the water in the deep shaft. The end of the cable was attached to the saddle on one of the pack mules.

Charvein felt a sense of relief, more for the animals than for the men. Once the outlaws had recovered from their thirst, they'd be harder to deal with.

He was impatient for the sun to dip behind the distant mountains; its rays shone directly into his eyes. He uncorked his canteen for a long drink and considered his next move. Now that water was no longer their main concern, the outlaws would turn their attention to finding food, then the gold. That hoard of precious metal had become the great mystery. Boyd must have thought it was hidden wherever he and his partners had stashed it. Yet it was no longer there. Charvein couldn't begin to guess where it had gone. He was not familiar with Lodestar or the area surrounding it. Had Boyd actually found the ingots and moved them to another hiding place so he could have it all? That would be consistent with his character. But had Boyd known the whereabouts, he likely would have revealed it under the tortured grilling administered by his former friends. Charvein concluded that Boyd was just as baffled by the gold's disappearance as the others.

Marc moved to the other side of the pile of spoil to get a better view of what the men were doing, since the noise and the voices had stopped. The animals still cropped the sparse vegetation, but the squealing pulley hung idle, and he saw no sign of the three men. He squinted into the setting sun.

"Hold it right there, mister!" came a sharp command.

Blinded by the sun, Charvein leapt to his right. Pumping a round into the chamber of his rifle, he fired. A scream of pain. A slug kicked up dirt inches from Charvein's foot. He couldn't see his assailant. Firing again, he dove for cover behind the pile. Blinking rapidly didn't clear the orange disks from his vision.

A bullet sang past his ear. He fired twice more as fast as he could pump the slide.

"Sumbitch shot me!" Weasel screamed.

"You ain't hit too bad or you couldn't yell that loud," Stepenaw's voice said. "Let's get him alive."

The clatter of boots running over rocks.

"I told you that warn't no ghost. Ghosts don't shoot real bullets."

"Shut up and help me!" Weasel screamed.

Charvein's sight was clearing, and he looked frantically for cover. He still had the pile of spoil between himself and the three. He fired around the edge twice more, trying to keep from exposing himself. His slugs slammed the side of the tin shed.

"Get down!"

While he had them ducking and Weasel wounded, Charvein bounded away, sprinting back down the wagon road. Within seconds, the bulge of the hill was protecting his back. His cover was blown, but he couldn't worry about that now.

Panting, he slipped and slid down the hill. In case they pursued, he didn't want to lead them to Sandoval and Lucy. If he could stay out of sight, they'd never track him over this rocky soil, especially with darkness coming on. He ducked and dodged, and made for a deep, narrow canyon choked with boulders where he could pick them off from a fortified position. Slipping into a cleft between the boulders, he breathed heavily while scanning the hillside. No one in sight. He proceeded to reload the rifle from his cartridge belt.

After several minutes he caught his breath, convinced he'd not misjudged these men. They had neither the courage nor the motivation to hunt him down. They didn't know who he was or why he was here. Even Boyd, who'd ambushed him, didn't know who he was. All they knew was that someone had taken their hostage, slugged Stepenaw, and left moccasin tracks. He had to assume Weasel had gotten a look at him just now, but Charvein had made him pay, clipping the man with a blind, lucky shot.

They now realized he was no ghost, that he was a stranger spying on them—that they'd have no peace until he was eliminated. Charvein smiled to himself. They were probably more confused than ever. Well, he'd keep them that way as long as he had his wits and weapons about him.

He eased out of the cleft and sat down with his back against a warm boulder, positioned where he could still see up the darkening hill. Sandoval had surely heard the shots, and Charvein hoped the man had sense enough not to come looking to see if he was in trouble.

Dusk grayed the shadowed canyon, pulling the blanket of another night over Lodestar. Nature continued to do what she'd always done—bake this remote corner of the planet with unforgiving sun, then blow dust over it by night.

As Sandoval had predicted, the night wind began to pick up. Although he couldn't feel it in his protected position, Charvein could hear it gusting across the hilltops above.

How bad was Weasel wounded? Charvein pictured the men working to fill their water containers before windy darkness closed down their operation and they had to get their animals to cover off the hilltop. They probably considered Charvein only a minor distraction they'd deal with later.

Finally deciding he was safe for the time being, Marc worked his way out of the rocks into the sandy wash in the bottom of the canyon. Greasewood and clumps of mesquite choked the canyon floor where rare runoff provided enough underground moisture for these desert plants to gain a foothold. The silence contrasted with the moaning wind above. He jogged along in the gathering dusk, planning to make a wide circle around the base of the mountain back to Sandoval's hiding place.

To avoid leaving footprints in the sand, he jumped from rock to rock. Glancing down at the last second as his right foot descended, he saw the thick body of a rattler coiled on a flat rock. He twisted in the air to avoid stepping on the snake, but too late. His weight landed on the rattler. With blurring speed, the head struck. Falling sideways, Charvein yanked his Colt and fired in one smooth motion. A sharp pain shot through his ankle as he came down awkwardly. The side of his head banged a boulder, shooting a spangle of lights across his vision before he blacked out.

NINE

Lucinda Barkley was finally beginning to feel human again. The terror of her abduction at gunpoint from the warden's office in Carson City, then the long, brutal horseback ride into the desert with little water and her hands bound to the saddle horn, followed by the fearful, suffocating dust storm—the whole nightmarish ordeal had caused her to despair. Exhausted, dehydrated, and benumbed, she'd nearly resigned herself to death by the time she and her captors had reached this ghost town.

Sitting atop a pile of blankets in Sandoval's cavern, she sipped at a canteen while she smelled the delicious aroma of cooking beans and meat. She was so dried out she didn't think her body could absorb enough water. Never again would she scorn water as the meanest of drinks. What had happened to her was hardly short of a miracle, she reflected. A stranger had appeared from nowhere and rescued her. When this man, who called himself Marc Charvein, had entered the saloon, he looked rougher than any of the others, and she feared some dark, bearded savage in high moccasins had come to slit her throat.

Perhaps it was her schooling in literature of the Middle Ages and the Renaissance that caused her to be so beguiled by European troubadours, wandering minstrels, the romantic intrigues of the French royal courts. Her head was full of poetic images of masked balls and handsome strangers who sang for their supper. Thus, it was against this backdrop that she compared her present adventures. She quickly put out of her mind the recent modern brutalities and hardships and pictured herself as a fair maiden in distress who'd been rescued by a handsome knight. In anticipation of returning home and regaling her friends with lurid tales of this experience, she polished details of the abduction, the ride, the hardships, the rescue. In actuality, with a shave and a bath, Marc Charvein would be quite handsome and could pass for a knight of centuries past. He even had a French name. She sighed, put her head down, and leaned forward on her knees. Oh well, perhaps she'd find the man of her dreams someday. She'd even settle for the man of someone else's dreams, if necessary. That's the way it worked in the French courts of old. Employment in Carson City was not her goal; San Francisco was, then maybe Paris. Time was flying, and she was a spinster at twenty-five.

She was still weak, but her appetite had returned, and she watched the Mexican move silently about the cavern, preparing food. She wondered about him. She'd spoken only a few words since her rescue, concentrating on drinking, obeying orders, and recovering her strength. This Sandoval said even less. What was he doing out here by himself in this deserted town? Her curiosity burned to know his story.

Sandoval stirred the pot that was imbedded in a layer of glowing coals at the entrance of the cavern. Then he scooped out a large spoonful of bacon and beans, folded a tortilla onto it, and handed the tin plate and spoon to her.

"Thank you." Her stomach growled at the aroma. She hadn't tasted food in nearly two days and nights.

Sandoval filled a plate for himself but suddenly stopped and cocked his head to one side. Setting his plate on the ground, he slid his long, open-top Colt from under his poncho and disappeared outside into the thick mesquite.

Sudden alarm lanced through Lucy's stomach. What was that noise? Several explosions?

A minute later, Sandoval returned, stony faced. His hooded eyes were fathomless. A slight flare of nostrils in his aquiline nose gave her the only clue to his emotion.

"What is it?" she ventured.

"Gunshots."

She waited for him to go on, and he finally said, "Several shots. Up the mountain. Not all the same gun."

She felt her eyes widening, her stomach tensing. What had happened? Was Marc in a fight with those men? Was he injured or—God forbid— killed? She set her food on the ground beside her.

Sandoval padded to the mouth of the cave again and paused alertly.

"Go see about him," she urged. "Don't worry about me. Just leave me one of your guns." She was proud of the words that seemed to flow out of her without reflection. She was indeed growing braver and more self-confident as a result of this whole ordeal.

It was the first time she'd seen any indecision on the part of this dark-skinned man. He looked at her, then back toward the entrance. Finally, he said, "If he has not returned by sunset, I will go look." He sat, cross-legged, and began to eat.

Lucy resumed her meal, not quite as hungry as before. An aura of danger and death was their silent supper companion.

When they finished eating, she heard a single, sharp report, this time much closer than the previous shots.

"A pistol," Sandoval said, getting up. "It is dusk. I will go see." His look seemed to plead for her understanding.

"I'll be fine," she repeated, forcing a smile. "I won't be caught unawares again," she added, thinking of her sudden capture during the prison break. She glanced toward the Henry rifle leaning against the wall.

Sandoval retrieved the rifle, then pulled his cartridge-conversion Colt and handed it to her, butt first. "This shoots true," he said. "Use it if anyone comes in besides me or Charvein. Just cock the hammer here and pull the trigger."

"I know how to use it," she said. Her father had made certain she was familiar with firearms before she sought a clerical job at the prison. He'd even bought her a derringer, but she'd neglected to carry it on that fateful day of the breakout.

Sandoval paused at the entrance and looked back. In the fading light, his obsidian eyes regarded her with what appeared to be more regret than concern. "Back soon."

One second he was there, and the next he was gone, and an oppressive, fearful silence reigned. She gripped the Colt, took a canteen, and moved back into the dark tunnel.

Sandoval knew Lodestar and the mountains that flanked it on the southwest side. Through the gathering dusk, he made his way quickly across the sloping flank of the mountain, eyes and ears keen as a lobo's, tracing the sound of the last shot he'd heard. He was certain it had come from a canyon just over a hundred paces from his cavern. He often hunted rabbits and other small game there and knew the area well. An uneasy feeling gripped him, and he'd long ago learned to trust his instincts. He crept forward past the old roadway to see down into the narrow defile, and dropped prone at the sight of two moving figures. Voices mumbled. Sandoval bellied forward and heard grunting as if the men were engaged in some kind of heavy work.

"That's it. Heave!"

"Hang on. Hang on. Put it down. I ain't got a good grip."

What were they carrying? A big sack of something heavy, it appeared. Should he fire and scare them off? Too dark to tell if it was two or three. He thought two. Where was the third? Better not shoot, or the third man, who was likely standing lookout, could gun him down.

"Okay, I got his feet."

With a start, Sandoval realized it was a body they were lugging. It had to be Charvein. If he was dead, were they hauling him to hide the body? But he might not be dead—only wounded. Darkness had snuffed Sandoval's chances of ambushing them successfully. He might accidentally hit Charvein. He'd also expose himself to return fire.

He could hear, more than see, the men stagger up the slope with their burden.

"Come on, the mule's only a little way," a voice said.

Sandoval rolled to his feet and moved away, scuffing small rocks as he did so, but the two workers were so absorbed in their task, they apparently didn't hear the stones rattling down the hill. The wind was beginning to gust.

He didn't want to leave Lucy alone too long, especially with the third man unaccounted for. He'd follow the sound in the night to see if the men were camping on the summit, near the source of their water. Then he'd return. The night wind he'd predicted tore at his long hair and peppered his eyes with grit as he crept cautiously up the old mining road, forty yards behind the men and the mule bearing the body of his new, and maybe late, friend.

TEN

Marc Charvein swam up from the depths of oblivion to the mumble of voices. He had no idea where he was or what had happened. While consciousness returned, he kept his eyes closed. The voices were familiar but were not those of Sandoval and Lucy. He recognized the nasal whine of Weasel. And, as the disjointed pieces of memory dropped into place, he knew he was in trouble. His stomach tightened, and he felt nauseous from the dull pain in his head. Lying on his back, he opened his eyes. Flickering firelight played across a rough rock ceiling ten feet above. Without moving his head, he shifted his glance toward the voices, but the sudden movement caused a sharp stab of pain behind his eyeballs. He closed his eyes, remained motionless, and listened.

"A waste of time and trouble haulin' him all the way here," Weasel said.

"You didn't do none o' the work," Stepenaw replied.

"You're takin' better care of him than you are of me."

Charvein imperceptibly moved his arms and legs—just

enough to find out if he was bound. He wasn't. How long had he been out? It was dark outside. He pressed his right arm against his side. As he'd expected, his gunbelt was missing. The last thing he remembered was bounding down the canyon, leaping from rock to rock. Then what? The snake. He'd tried to avoid landing on a coiled rattler. Twisting sideways, he'd lost his balance. As he went down, he got off a snap shot at the snake. Then he blacked out. Had the fangs struck him in the leg? He went cold with dread at the idea, but dared not move to check himself. He blocked out the thought and focused on the nearby conversation.

". . . griping all the time," Stepenaw was saying. "Worse than that woman we had with us."

"His bullet busted my damn arm!"

"Too bad it wasn't your flappin' jaw."

Weasel muttered something, then said, "Better be a damned good reason you're treatin' him like an invited guest."

"There is," Stepenaw said. "See those moccasins he's wearing? He's the one took our hostage, so now we got *him* for a replacement."

"If he lives, that is," a third voice said.

After a moment, Charvein realized it was Boyd speaking.

"If he don't wake up, then he's food for the buzzards," Stepenaw said.

Charvein could hear the big man moving around. He peeked through his eyelashes and saw sparks swirling upward as someone stirred the campfire.

"Reckon we oughta see to him. He ain't no good to us dead," Stepenaw said.

"Gawd! This arm o' mine pains me. Loosen this wrap some; I think there ain't no blood getting to my fingers."

Charvein sensed someone approaching.

"You sumbitch!"

Charvein gasped as a boot toe caught him in the ribs. It took all the willpower he had not to move or cry out.

"Here, now!" Stepenaw thundered. "Leave him be. He's our insurance. If you can't take a little pain, you should never've joined up with us in the first place."

"I want to find out who he is," Boyd said. "He sure as hell looks familiar somehow. I've seen that face somewhere lately."

Charvein wondered how long he should fake unconsciousness. He'd almost given himself away when Weasel kicked him. He wasn't afraid of being in the hands of the enemy as much as he feared the effects of the serpent's fangs. Was poison coursing through his body even now? But he felt no numbness or pain. The men would surely have mentioned it—unless they'd heard his shot and come upon him when he was already out cold, and hadn't bothered to identify his injuries.

"Well, I reckon this flesh-and-blood man proves there's no ghost in this town, like you two believed." Boyd snorted a laugh.

"There's lots of things in this world you don't know nothing about," Weasel shot back. "Lots o' things nobody understands. There's a spirit world out there we can't see."

Boyd chuckled, which seemed to infuriate Weasel.

"The Injuns live close to the land and animals, and they know about such things!" he ranted.

"You reckon this fella's Injun?" Stepenaw wondered. "He's wearing them moccasins. They look to be Apache."

"See that growth of whiskers?" Boyd said. "He ain't no Indian. If anything, he's a breed. Reckon most of that dark skin is from sun and dirt."

Charvein identified the pain in his head as radiating from one very sore spot high on his left temple.

"I'm starved. Let's eat," Stepenaw said.

Charvein sniffed the aroma of roasting meat and his stomach growled. Maybe it was time to quit faking unconsciousness. He opened his eyes again. Acrid smoke was drifting near the ceiling, stirred by a breeze from the mouth of the cave. He moved and rolled over on his side, with a groan.

"Well, he's back to life," Stepenaw said.

A red, unshaven face appeared in Charvein's vision. He pushed himself to a sitting position, and closed his eyes while a wave of dizziness passed. He felt hung over and remembered why he'd quit drinking ten years ago. He got to one knee then, unsteadily, to his feet.

"Don't try nuthin'," Stepenaw said, taking a step back and drawing his Colt.

"He's not armed, remember?" Boyd said.

"Don't matter. He's a slick one."

"You still think he's some kind of ghost, don't you?" Boyd chuckled. "Does a spirit bleed? Look at that cut on his head."

Charvein instinctively touched his head with his fingertips. A tender, walnut-size lump, with crusty blood. The muzziness he felt must be the result of a mild concussion, he guessed. He hoped his skull wasn't cracked. "Where're my guns?"

"Unloaded and stashed safely away," Boyd replied. "Anybody who can blast the head off a rattlesnake had best not be playing with loaded guns. Somebody might get hurt. And that somebody might be us." He gave a tight smile as his eyes squinted at Charvein through the smoke. "Reckon your head's a mite harder than that boulder," Boyd went on. "Figured you for a goner when we first gathered you up."

"Didn't mean you boys no harm," Charvein said, trying the stupid, innocent, conciliatory approach first.

"Like hell!" Weasel snapped, holding his forearm.

"I was trying to get a look at you up at that old mine," Charvein continued, "but the sun got in my eyes. Thought you was about to blast me, so I let loose. Instinct. Couldn't even see what I was shooting at."

"That story won't wash, mister," Stepenaw growled, still holding his Colt level. He thumbed back the hammer, as if expecting Charvein to spring at him.

"Did the snake get me?" Charvein asked to change the subject. He ran both hands down his pants legs.

"Watch it!" Weasel warned. "He could have a hideout gun in the tops of them moccasins."

"I searched him," Boyd said. "He's clean."

Charvein raised his hands away from the moccasins.

"You'd know it by now if that rattler got you," Boyd said. "You been out a good two hours."

"Where are we, anyway?" Charvein asked.

"One of the caves in Nightwind Canyon," Boyd said.

For the first time, Charvein became aware of the wind buffeting the small bushes just outside the cave entrance. An eerie, undulating howling came from without, like someone blowing into the neck of an empty bottle, only a thousand times louder.

"Don't reckon it's called 'Nightwind Canyon' for nothing," Charvein said. "Sounds rough out there." He took a deep breath and then scrubbed a hand over the stubble on his cheeks. "I appreciate you boys looking after me, but I'm feeling some better now, so I won't trouble you no further. I'll just take my guns and be on my way."

"You ain't going nowhere, mister; we ain't done with you," Stepenaw said. "Just have a set-down over there by the wall and get comfortable, 'cause I got some questions I want answered." He motioned with the Colt.

"Wish you'd let the hammer down on that thing nice and easy," Charvein held up both palms toward the outlaw. "I'd hate for it to go off, accidental-like."

"So would I, 'cause if it goes off it won't be no accident." The big man attempted a grin, showing tobacco-stained teeth.

Charvein eased himself to the hard floor and leaned his back against the rock wall, glancing longingly at the irregular cave entrance several yards away. It might have been a mile away. Should he continue to play dumb? Were these men killers as well as armed robbers and escapees? He'd have to be cagey. Desperate men do desperate things, and he assumed they were capable of murder. He'd try to placate them, and lie his way out of this. They might be gullible enough to believe some cock-and-bull story made up on the moment and just let him go as harmless. Trouble was, he had no practice lying, never having had a poker face. Besides, if they needed a hostage in case of pursuit, they'd hold him prisoner regardless.

"Time for talk after we eat," Boyd said, a little too amiably. "Since you supplied the vittles, you want a bite?"

It was then Charvein realized that the small chunks of white meat they'd spitted on sticks over the fire were roasting rattlesnake.

He shook his head slowly. "Feeling a bit sick just now from this knock on the head," he said, truthfully. If they were eating the snake he'd shot, and nothing else, they must be short of grub. What would be their next move, come daylight? "As long as you're being so hospitable, I could use some of that coffee, though. Might ease this headache."

"I'll give you a goddamned headache!" Weasel muttered, continuing to glare at him.

Boyd poured a tin cup of steaming coffee and handed it to Charvein.

The men used their belt knives to spear and eat the hot bites of rattlesnake.

In the few minutes of silence as supper proceeded, Charvein sipped the bitter brew and listened to the night wind howl its strange lament. Sandoval had said Nightwind Canyon was less than a mile from town. But which direction? West or southwest, Charvein thought. Even if he could somehow slip outside into the darkness, he didn't know which way to run or dodge to elude pursuit. Just now, he didn't feel like trying a break. Most likely get shot for his trouble. Weasel, especially, would have no compunction about pumping a bullet into his hide—if he got a chance. For the moment, Charvein concentrated on devising a cover story to explain who he was and how he happened to be here. It had to sound convincing. Even if they didn't believe him, he'd keep up his bluff and stick to his story.

Boyd finished the last of his snake and wiped his fingers on his trousers as he sat cross-legged on the stone floor. "Now, then, why don't you tell us about yourself, mister, and why you're in Lodestar." His voice was civil, almost courteous, but Charvein recalled the .50-caliber slugs that had killed his horse and nearly himself. This man was capable of anything and could afford to be civil; he was in total control. A strange situation. The two escapees had tortured Boyd. But later, in their common need for water, had called a truce and given him back his pistol but apparently not the long-barreled Sharps. Now Boyd had assumed his natural position of leadership. In truth, he appeared much smarter than the other two. Yet, technically, Boyd was still their prisoner.

Charvein bluffed an attitude of friendly eagerness to tell his story. "Lost my job as a carpenter in Gold Hill," he began. "I was riding across the playa, thinking to do some prospecting in these mountains. Figured there might be some likely looking ore hereabouts." He paused and touched the lump on the side of his skull that was throbbing. "I'd heard about this ghost town. Even if I didn't strike any good prospects, I aimed to work over the tailings at the old mines. They're bound to've missed some nuggets here and there in these big operations." He tried his best to look muddled. He'd finished his coffee but was still thirsty. His full canteen still lay beside him, so he uncorked it and took a long drink.

"Ahhh!" He wiped his mouth with the back of his hand.

"Quit stalling!" Boyd snapped.

"Well, as I said, I figured there must be some bits of ore scattered around that these big mines missed years ago when they moved out. Ya know, not enough to support a commercial operation, but plenty good enough to keep a poor fella like me going."

"You already said that."

"Yeah, well . . . I was riding across the playa couple days ago headed this way and some sumbitch dry-gulched me— shot my horse and damn near got me, too. Some robber, I reckon. Don't know why anybody'd think I had anything to steal." He pretended not to notice Boyd compressing his lips. The man's eyes narrowed as if trying to read the truth behind Charvein's pose.

Charvein dropped his eyes and continued. "Damn near died in that dust storm—just like the one blowin' outside right now." He gestured toward the cave opening. "Didn't think I was gonna make it. Never been that thirsty. Lost my direction and . . ."

"You're windier than that damn storm," Boyd said. "Get on with it."

Charvein nodded. "Finally passed out. When I woke up at daylight I found myself right on the edge of this town. Dumb luck, I reckon."

"Where'd you get food and water?" Boyd interrupted.

"Searched these old buildings and found a bottle of sarsaparilla. Shot a jackrabbit . . ."

"Where'd you get that canteen of water?"

Charvein thought fast. "Carried it with me. The last of six I started with. The only thing I salvaged off my dead horse, besides my pistol and rifle."

"How you figuring to survive?" Boyd asked.

Charvein shrugged. "Live off the land as best I could. I raked over a few piles of spoil, but didn't have no luck finding any good ore. Then I hid when you boys hit town. Didn't know what to expect. Thought maybe you was the ones who shot at me earlier." He slid over this statement as if it were a remote possibility. "I saw you boys getting water outta that mine from the hoisting works up top the hill there and decided I'd slip up and spy on you—you know—to see if I could tell if you was friendly and all. I had to find more water and a way back to Virginia City. Looked like you might be my only chance. Then, this skinny fella jumped me and I was blinded by the sun, like I said, and I just fired. Got scared and ran off, figuring you'd shoot me. Well . . . you know the rest . . ."

For a minute, the three men stared silently at him. The wind roared down the canyon, mournfully howling past the cave opening. Had his story carried any authenticity? The part about the ambush was true, so maybe they'd believe the rest of it.

"Now you gonna tell us the part you left out?" Boyd asked. He drew his revolver and placed it suggestively in his lap. Charvein could see the chambers were empty. His former partners didn't trust Boyd with a loaded weapon. It was now Boyd's turn to bluff.

"What part?" Charvein tried to look bewildered.

"How you stole that woman outta the saloon."

He shook his head. "Don't get your drift. What woman?"

Stepenaw sprang forward with a speed and agility that belied his size and backhanded Charvein across the face. He saw it coming at the last instant but couldn't avoid the blow. His head snapped sideways. A bright light flashed. For a second he thought he might black out. But he pushed himself upright, his head spinning. He tasted salty blood.

"Enough of that!" Boyd snapped.

"That's for slugging me in the head when I wasn't looking," Stepenaw growled as he stepped back.

"Slug . . . you?" Charvein hoped his face showed total ignorance.

"That improve your memory any?" Weasel gloated.

Charvein now wished he'd taken time to rub out the prints of his moccasins on the dusty saloon floor. But there'd been no chance, since the men were returning. He and the woman had barely escaped unseen.

"You can beat me all night, but I can't tell you what I don't know," Charvein said. His head was really throbbing now. How much more could he take? They didn't buy his story completely. It was going to be a long night.

ELEVEN

"He's where?" Lucy's voice carried a combined tone of hope and despair.

"In Nightwind Canyon," Sandoval replied. "One of the caves." Noting her look of grief, he added, "I'm sure he is alive, or they would not bother with him." He shook his head. "I don't know how badly he is hurt, but he was still unconscious when they pulled him off the mule and carried him inside." He watched her reaction. She seemed stricken, as if for an injured husband or lover. The women he'd known in the past had always baffled him with their emotional, inconsistent behavior. This one was no different. She barely knew Charvein.

"Where is Nightwind Canyon?"

"A mile or more southwest of here. Not sure why they camped there; they were already set up in the Red Horse Saloon. Probably better protection from the wind and dust." He had another theory but kept it to himself.

"Why do these men want him? Who are they, anyway? Why are they all in this ghost town?"

Sandoval took these as rhetorical questions, since she'd been present when the men were arguing about the location of the gold and torturing Boyd to find it. She was only frustrated and angry and had to say something.

"When you were a captive, did you hear them say where they were headed or why?" he asked.

She shook her head slowly. "No . . . They seemed more worried about a posse coming after them and pushed hard to get far away from Carson to hide in the mountains." She furrowed her brow. "No, wait . . . I did hear the one they call Weasel say something about Lodestar. I didn't know then it was the name of a town. They mentioned they might run into their old partner. But I was so far gone with hunger and thirst, I wasn't really listening to their conversation."

Sandoval motioned for her to take a seat on the blanket near the small campfire by the screened entrance to the cavern. It wouldn't hurt to fill her in on what details he knew of these three men. He added a few small sticks to the fire and reflected on how he might have avoided getting involved in all this. His solitude had been shattered, and he could see no way it might not have occurred. In spite of his constant vigilance, unforeseen things happened. He was a fool to think his life here could go on uninterrupted forever. Of course, he could have left Charvein to die of thirst and exposure at the edge of town the other night. But that wasn't his way. And he would still have the three outlaws to deal with. What was done was done.

"I do not know if Marc Charvein told you any of this, but he's tracking that man named Boyd, in hopes of locating the gold those three stole five years ago."

"Yes," she nodded. "The warden was very upset when the governor pardoned Boyd a couple of weeks ago."

"Boyd was released early, so he's not really a fugitive. But he could be arrested again if he's caught with somebody else's gold." He poked at the fire and it flared up briefly, reflecting tears brimming in Lucy's eyes.

"So the two men who escaped and kidnapped me are Boyd's partners and want their share of the gold."

"Yes." He paused, at a loss for anything to say that might comfort her. "I hope Charvein makes up some story to cover himself." He reached for a bottle on a rock shelf just inside the entrance. He yanked the cork with his teeth, then spat it to one side and took a long swallow. It went down smoothly, silently exploding in his gut. Cheap to make and entirely too available, he thought. He hadn't taken a drink in weeks. Probably not a good idea to start now, but he justified it as medicine to calm his nerves and help him sleep. He silently offered a drink to Lucy, but she shook her head. He recorked the bottle and returned it to the shelf. "Charvein strikes me as smart. He'll do what he can to keep them from discovering why he's here. But I'm afraid no matter what he says, they'll just use him as a convenient hostage."

"Do you think the law will somehow follow them here?" she asked.

He shrugged. "They think so, or they wouldn't bother keeping a hostage."

"What can we do?" Her tone was plaintive. "He saved me; we have to save him."

Sandoval had been pondering much the same thing. But no ready solution presented itself. "You hungry?" he asked to divert the question.

"No."

Then he realized it hadn't even been two hours since they'd eaten. They sat silently for a minute, staring into the low flames and entertaining their own thoughts.

"Another heavy wind outside," she commented.

Sandoval nodded, only half-aware of the mesquite bushes thrashing a few yards away. He was mulling over

ways he might take advantage of the darkness, the dust, and
the howling wind in Nightwind Canyon. Surely there was
some way to make use of the cover the storm provided.

Their conversation lagged. The fire slowly died to a bed
of coals winking red in the fitful breeze that found its way
inside.

Lucy began to nod.

"Rest," he said. "You must be worn out."

"I'll just stretch out here and close my eyes for a minute," she said, not moving away from him or the dying fire.

Sandoval guessed it was near midnight. The wind continued unabated. "Lucy, I have an idea. I'm going out for a
while." He paused as she stirred in the darkness. "I should
be back in an hour or two. If something happens and I don't
get back, you have food and water here, and you have my
mule and burro to get back to Carson City."

"Where are you going?"

"I have a plan that might distract those men so they'll
forget about Charvein, and we can get him free."

"Oh, be careful," she said. "I don't know what I'd do if I
lost both of you."

He needed no light as he moved to the back of the cavern
and opened a wooden box. He filled the two inside pockets
of his poncho. Returning, he crouched beside her, a full
canteen slung over one shoulder. He gripped his Henry
rifle. "This could take me a little longer than I first thought.
Don't fret if I don't return until after daylight. As long as
you stay here and be quiet, you'll be all right. Don't stir up
that fire. Give my animals some grain and water."

"Yes, yes," she said. "I'll do as you say." Her voice
sounded more assured and less anxious. "*Adios,*" he heard
her whisper as he slipped outside into the screening bosque.

TWELVE

Ex–Deputy Marshal Buck Rankin was sorely tempted to take French leave. Hunkered under a blanket on the lee side of his horse, he impatiently endured the gusting wind and suffocating dust of the playa. Advancing years had made him soft; he'd let this posse of volunteers drag him to a stop before he was ready. Now they were spending another night exposed to the elements on this dry lake bed. If they'd kept going at sunset as he urged, they could have reached the nearest desert mountains before the worst of the night wind began to howl.

Unable to sleep, he was being tormented by the incessant buffeting of dust that powdered the insides of his nostrils, clogged his nose, grated between his teeth, and worked its way inside his collar. It left a bitterness in his mouth and attitude. He fought the urge to jump up and run screaming into the night, cursing this damnable weather, his companions, and his luck. His was not a passive nature. Endurance was not his forte; action was.

The men huddled in their blankets. The hobbled horses

stood, rumps to the wind, manes and tails whipping in the relentless gusts. Rankin wondered if any of the men were asleep. For the plan he was formulating, they had to be. He was going to shed himself of this posse. They weren't man hunters. They could only slow him down. And if it came to a showdown, they'd bungle the job, get in the way, and maybe get him killed. He'd purposely bedded down fifteen yards upwind from the nearest member of the posse. No sign of life came from any of them. The last time he'd struck a match under his blanket to check his watch, it was 12:40 A.M. And that was at least an hour ago. It was time to make his move. So what if he abandoned these men in the middle of a dust storm? Come morning, they'd gripe and moan, but they had water and food enough to see them back to town, even though it'd probably take them two days—as much as they liked to rest themselves and their horses.

Only one man of the posse was he unsure of, one who had a mean streak as wide as the yellow streaks of the others—a mean streak that might pass for courage in a fight. Schooner Douglas was a big, rawboned Scotsman who ran a saloon in Gold Hill and was probably his own best customer. Taken away for a few days or weeks from his favorite beverage, Schooner tended to get mean. He'd killed more than one man in a rough-and-tumble fight, so the story went. Buck suspected the saloonkeeper had stashed a bottle or two in his saddlebags, but so far there'd been no indication Schooner was nipping. Buck had made it clear he'd tolerate no drinking on the job.

Like the others, Schooner Douglas stood to collect a considerable reward if these men were either captured or killed. And Douglas was not the kind of man to throw up his hands and head home once he saw that their leader had left them stranded. As far as needing a share of the reward, Douglas had a business that appeared to bring in a goodly flow of money, whereas, he, Buck Rankin, broken-down ex-marshal, had only a tiny pension. The way his leg felt, this could be his last manhunt as a freelancer. He had to earn all he could—now. There was no tomorrow or next month or next year. He was not feeling pity for himself; leave that to lesser men. He was only calculating the cold, hard facts. By gathering in all the reward from the state and from the wealthy relatives of the woman hostage, he'd have a cushion of several thousand in the bank, enough to set himself up in a small business. He had no intention of dying in poverty. No, siree. He had his wits and his guns, and he intended to finish this job on his own. He would never have brought along these citizen volunteers except at the insistence of the sheriff who thought he was doing Buck a good turn by supplying their help. Well, by God, the sheriff apparently had the same low opinion of him as most others did: a good lawman in his day, but his day was done. Buck had never been one to care much what folks thought about him.

He drew his legs under him, cringing at the old injury in the back of his thigh. Throwing back the protective blanket, he forced himself to stand, stretching his hamstring. Was it his imagination, or was the wind lessening?

Now that he'd made up his mind to finish this manhunt alone, he was impatient to be off. Wherever the outlaws were, they must have gone to ground in this dust storm. If he could be on the move now, he'd gain precious time and distance on them. They surely wouldn't be expecting anyone to come at them out of this dry hurricane. He had to use all advantages, surprise being one of the best. If they put up a fight, he'd shoot to kill without hesitation.

His bad leg was paining him something fierce, so there was no time to lose, no time to drag this deadweight posse behind him.

In total darkness, and with his back to the wind, he could see nothing of his companions. He removed the protective slicker he'd tucked in loosely around the horse's headstall. Operating more by touch than sight, he tightened the cinch straps, unclipped the hobbles, and rolled and tied his blanket behind the saddle. Then he grasped the reins and led his mount away, the wind masking any small sounds.

He figured Lodestar was a few miles directly west. The quartering wind was coming from the southwest at a forty-five-degree angle to his heading.

After a few steps, he glanced back. His companions were swallowed up in blackness as if they'd never existed. He hoped the wind wasn't veering, since he'd have to walk at a constant angle to it in order to maintain course; he couldn't be stopping every hundred yards to huddle under his blanket and strike a match to check his compass. This would be like dead-reckoning navigation at sea.

His horse hated it even more than he did, continually pulling to the side, trying to turn his back to the blowing dust. Rankin tied a bandanna across his own nose and mouth and partially protected his eyes with a pair of green-tinted glasses he'd originally brought along to cut the glare of the sun. Since he couldn't see where he was going anyway, it didn't matter how dark the lenses were.

The horse fought the lead with every step, so Rankin finally stopped and took his spare shirt from the saddlebag. He tied its soft cotton arms around the animal's head to keep out the wind and dust, tucking the loose ends inside the headstall to keep them from flapping. This would have the effect of blinders in calming the animal.

He slogged on, head down, wind bending his hat brim.

He wondered how much dust was getting into his lungs. Was the powdered soil any worse than breathing cigar smoke in a saloon?

"Buck Rankin!"

The distant shout of his own name jarred him for a moment. But then he realized it probably came from inside his own head. "Yeah, Buck Rankin," he said aloud, "you're tougher than any of 'em."

"Raannkin!" A wavering cry he barely heard.

Startled, he stopped dead, turning his head this way and that, listening. Surely some trick of the wind. This strange place, this scorched, abandoned tip of the planet, was getting to him. He was drying out. That was it: dehydrated and hearing things. He fumbled for the canteen that hung from the saddle horn. Pulling down the bandanna, he tipped up the canteen and took a long drink.

"Raaankin! Wait!"

He yanked the canteen from his lips, sputtering and half-choking on a swallow. That wasn't the wind or his imagination. This time the sound had seemed to come from off to one side. But he couldn't be sure. He wiped a sleeve across his mouth.

"Why you running, Rankin?"

He whirled around to face the voice that came from the west, from upwind. A prickly chill ascended his back to his hairline. The wind could create ghostly sounds, but it absolutely could not mimic the sound of his name, over and over again. In fact, there were no obstructions—not even a bush or rock—that could divert the wind and cause any sort of unusual noise. Somebody was out there, playing a trick on him. He dismissed the idea that this could be his conscience. A completely practical man, Rankin didn't believe in such things. But madness? He'd seen men go mad, and he knew that insanity was a fact. It happened. But not to him. His mind had always been stable. He'd never taken drugs, or been a drunk, or gone through any horrifying ordeal like being trapped without food and water for days in a mine or the mountains—things that might send a man over the mental edge of reality.

He pulled up the bandanna, took up the reins, and resolutely put the sounds out of his mind as he trudged westward into the gusting wind. The strange cries ceased and his uneasiness slowly ebbed while he fought the elements. His laboring breath dampened the bandanna and the dust stuck to it, turning to mud. But he didn't stop, didn't slow down. It seemed an hour dragged away. Pain elongated time, so he guessed it was more like thirty minutes. Had he gone a mile? Two miles?

Finally, he pulled up, stopping for a moment of rest. He untied the shirt from the horse's head to make sure the animal was all right. Glancing back the way he'd come, he noted a blurry dimness that heralded the coming dawn. He'd never been so glad to see daylight coming. He had a greater appreciation of how blind people were able to function in a dark world.

He shook out the shirt and started tying it back in place.

"Buck!"

He jumped and whirled toward the voice. No one.

"Runnin' out, Rankin?" The ridicule was evident. Now he knew that voice—Schooner Douglas.

"Shit! Show yourself, you son of a bitch!" Rankin yelled, though his voice came out as a hoarse croak. "Dammit, Schooner, face up like a man." The gusts whisked his words away. He knew his voice carried no more than a few feet.

Suddenly, the figure of a big man rose up, silhouetted against the pale eastern sky. Fear stabbed Rankin's gut. He snatched off the green-tinted spectacles and flung them away, grabbing for his holstered gun. The six-gun jumped in his fist; the explosions of three quick shots were some-how reassuring. He was fighting something besides a ghost. Somewhere beyond the muzzle flashes, the figure vanished. Though he'd been sighting through irritated eyes, Rankin knew his shots were true. But maybe the figure wasn't; if it was a man, he'd dropped out there with three bullets in him. Schooner Douglas, be damned!

His heart was pounding now, and he yanked down the bandanna, coughing as he breathed in the dust. Watering eyes scanned the gradually lightening scene. Blurring emptiness. "A dust devil—that's what you are—a dust devil. A whirlwind, a column of dust that looks like a man," he croaked, starting to doubt his sanity.

Again he staggered toward the west. Sweat burst from every pore, soaking his clothes. Terrified and disoriented, he didn't realize for a minute that his horse had bolted at the sound of his gunfire and galloped off, vanishing into the murk. Never mind; he'd find the big sorrel when daylight came.

Sometime later, he felt the ground rising under his boot soles, as if he were wading up out of a lake. Through gritty eyes, he thought he could make out a jumble of buildings ahead. But now he doubted his own senses. Nothing was real.

He could hardly breathe; he felt as if he were suffocating. Then he heard the mellow tolling of a bell. A slow, deep, muffled tone. The thought crossed his mind that he was late for his own funeral. He had to hurry; they'd be expecting him. Blindly striving for whatever was up ahead, he moved his legs automatically, the familiar ache in his right hamstring telling him he was still among the living. Dead men felt no pain. He plunged ahead.

Suddenly, they were there—the dried, brown, sagging buildings of Lodestar, rattling and banging in the wind. He twisted to look behind. He'd escaped the playa. He'd shot the specter who'd been stalking him. Or maybe he'd just shot *at* something and scared it off—some creature of the playa who'd come out of the dark and dust to prey on solo travelers. He realized his thinking was askew, but he couldn't seem to get his head straightened out.

The back door of the first building stood ajar. He pushed it open and went inside. Suddenly relieved from the need to lean against the wind, he lost his balance and fell to the wooden floor. He didn't care where he was, as he gulped the relatively clear air. His head was whirling. He'd made it to Lodestar. "I'll just rest a bit," he told himself in a whisper, "then go look for m'horse." He took a deep breath. "Finally rid o' that damned posse." And he drifted into unconsciousness.

THIRTEEN

"Hell, tie him up if you think he's going to escape," Boyd said to Stepenaw. "But stop waving that damned gun around. You're making me nervous."

"Hold this while I put some ropes on him."

Weasel took the Colt in his good hand.

Charvein submitted meekly, still playing the role of innocence.

Stepenaw used his braided hemp lariat to bind Charvein's hands together in front of him, then bent him forward to tie wrists to ankles. Only when Charvein was lying on his side, trussed and helpless, did Stepenaw accept his Colt from Weasel and holster it.

Boyd lounged on his blanket near the fire, watching. "That's better. Now we can all relax." He dragged his saddlebags toward him. "Got a little surprise here," he said, loosening the strap and thrusting a hand inside. "Was planning to save it to celebrate when we found the gold, but since it's disappeared, I reckon it won't hurt to break it out now." He held aloft a quart bottle of Noble's whiskey. "Besides," he continued, twisting out the cork, "Weasel could likely use a good, stiff drink to dull the pain in that arm."

"By God, you been holding out on us," Weasel said, licking his lips. "Probably holding out about the gold, too, but first things first."

The rich, amber liquid glowed warm in the firelight.

Charvein, lying on his side by the wall, watched Boyd pour a generous amount into each man's tin cup.

The wounded man and his big companion tipped up their drinks.

"Whew! That's good!" Weasel's grimace seemed to belie his words. He drained his cup and held it out for a refill. Boyd complied.

Stepenaw merely smacked his lips, grunted, then attacked the drink again, his massive hands engulfing the tin cup. He also got a refill.

"Ain't you having none?" Weasel asked, eyeing Boyd, who was recorking the bottle.

"I'll take a nip before bedtime," he replied, "to help me sleep. I have to go easy on the hard stuff; it upsets my stomach when I haven't had much to eat." He smiled and poured himself half a cup of coffee and leaned back against his saddle.

Charvein suspected the crafty Boyd was up to something. He wondered where the men had left their horses and mules. Surely they hadn't been picketed outside in the dust storm. The tin-sided sheds on the hilltop couldn't have been used for the animals since the wind rattled and banged the loose metal. There must be other caves nearby, possibly the openings in the walls were like the holes in a flute and caused the eerie moaning and crying of the night wind in this aptly named canyon. Charvein wasn't thirsty or hungry, but his untreated head still ached. He was glad Stepenaw had not tied his hands behind his back, a position that would have made sleep impossible. At least partially doubled over like this he might be able to doze off and get some rest. He wiggled his hands and feet to test his bonds.

The oiled hemp was around his shirt cuffs and his moccasins, so the rope didn't chafe, and it wasn't so tight as to restrict blood circulation. He'd remain quiet and try to sleep. Maybe the morning would bring a chance for escape.

The untended fire slowly burned down to only a few flickers of flame.

The liquor loosened Weasel's tongue, and he babbled on about the missing gold and where it might be, cursing Boyd for retrieving it and hiding it. He finally stretched out on his blanket, continuing to mumble, slurring his words. The others ignored him.

Stepenaw got quietly drunk, helping himself to another cupful from the bottle lying near Boyd's saddlebags. The small pieces of rattlesnake meat hadn't been a full meal for any of them, and there wasn't enough food in their stomachs to absorb much of the alcohol. In his years as a peace officer, Charvein had dealt with many drunken men. Even hardened drinkers, given physical work and very little rest, would succumb to straight whiskey rather quickly. A man of Stepenaw's size could soak up more, but it finally began to affect him as well.

Time dragged like a flat-sided wheel. Weasel was stretched on his blanket, unconscious. Stepenaw began to nod, then drooped to an awkward position, lying on one arm, still holding his cup. Boyd continued to sip his coffee, half-closed eyes watching, catlike.

The cave grew darker. The fire collapsed into ash-covered coals, winking a red eye every few seconds as the light air fanned it. Charvein could no longer see Boyd.

An anguished moaning, almost humanlike, rose and fell outside, the wind and grit scouring the canyon. The sound was punctuated by Stepenaw's ragged snoring and snorting.

Sometime later, in spite of his restricted position, weariness stole over Charvein and he dozed off to strange, disjointed dreams. He dreamed Sandoval was calling him, and he tried to answer, but the wind drowned his voice. That scene faded, and he heard the woman crying. She had again been captured, and the men were getting uproariously drunk to celebrate. Charvein tried to go to her rescue but didn't have his gun, and he couldn't lift his arms or legs.

He gasped and woke himself with a snort, clammy with perspiration as the dream vanished and the reality of the ropes reappeared. He took several deep breaths to calm himself, doubting he'd be able to recapture sleep. He desperately needed to shift his position to stretch his arms, legs, and back.

Suddenly, his heart missed a beat. He'd sensed something moving within a foot of him—probably some animal taking shelter in this cave. He had opened his mouth to yell out a warning to Boyd, when a hand was clamped over his mouth, stifling his shout. He struggled.

"Shsst! Keep still!" Boyd's voice whispered urgently.

Charvein stopped struggling and waited.

"I'm cutting you loose," the voice said, close to his ear.

Boyd fumbled for the bound wrists and ankles. Charvein felt cold steel slide under the ropes, and in a few seconds, they were slashed and fell away. Boyd gripped his arm, helping him up. Charvein leaned over with a sudden attack of dizziness as blood rushed out of his head. Boyd waited, then led him in the blackness along the wall to the entrance. What next? Was he being taken outside to be shot? If Boyd wanted to kill him, he could have done it with a silent knife thrust while he lay bound.

They walked ten steps from the cave entrance, while the wind tore at their clothes and hair. No need now to talk in whispers.

"What's this?" Charvein asked, feeling a gunbelt thrust into his hands.

"Get out of here and don't come back," Boyd said in a barely audible voice. "Your gun's not loaded, but there are cartridges in the belt loops. You'll have to do without your rifle. I'm taking it, since those two have my Sharps." He was silent for a moment and Charvein averted his face from the flying grit that whipped around them. Boyd stepped closer and raised his voice slightly to be heard. "Get out of town with that woman. I can't spare any animals. You're on your own."

Charvein wanted to question the man, to ask the reason for this rescue. But he knew. Boyd owed nothing to his former partners who'd disarmed and tortured him, kept him a virtual prisoner. And there was no telling what the two drunks inside the cave had planned once morning came. This was Boyd's revenge—and his escape.

With that, the voice ceased, and Charvein squinted into the darkness that had swallowed up his benefactor. "Wait! Which way is Lodestar?" No answer. "Shit!" He quickly buckled on his gunbelt and paused a half minute to load his Colt. The prevailing wind was from the southwest, so the town had to be somewhere to his right. He moved out thirty steps from the canyon wall, then bore right to give the unseen cave entrance plenty of clearance. He felt secure. Befuddled with drink, the two were likely still deeply asleep. He smiled. Boyd apparently knew his former partners well; their weakness for whiskey made the escape easy.

He tied a bandanna across his nose and mouth and felt his way forward, stumbling over rocks and small bushes, making slow progress. But then he worked his way back to the nearly vertical canyon wall, keeping it to his right to be sure he didn't walk in circles. After two falls, his injured head was throbbing. How far had he gone? How much farther? In the darkness and windblown dust, time and distance could not be measured. Would the two outlaws awake to find both him and Boyd gone and start a hunt? After tripping and scraping his hand, Charvein rested on one knee. Weasel had a broken arm, and the two of them had taken on a load of booze. Even if they came to, they'd likely be too hungover to mount a useful search in the dark. Boyd had two mules and might also steal the escapees' two mounts and Lucy's horse, setting the pair afoot. Charvein grinned at the thought. He, himself, had only his two feet, but they were encased in Apache desert moccasins.

An hour passed, and the night wind slackened. Although he couldn't be sure, he took this as a sign dawn was approaching. He was right. Dim light stole into the canyon, like the infusion of clear water into a jar of cloudy liquid. At first Charvein could dimly make out the rugged canyon wall, then boulders strewn along the sloping floor. The light seemed to come faster. Before long he could distinguish details of shrubs and see ahead where the canyon flattened out. Beyond that, Lodestar's abandoned buildings thrust their rectangular shapes above the settling dust.

He yanked down his bandanna and paused to get his breath. He wondered if Boyd would give up his quest for the stolen gold and return to Virginia City, waiting until Stepenaw and Weasel were gone before returning. With the town of Lodestar again empty—as far as he knew—he could return to search for the stolen stash.

Charvein knew his mission was finished. Boyd was gone, and the gold was still missing. He'd find Sandoval, borrow his mule and sufficient water to escort Lucy back to Carson City, then report his failure to his employer in Virginia City. It was as simple as that. Of course, in his escape from Lodestar, he might have to defend them both against Stepenaw and the wounded Weasel. But, considering all he'd been through so far, he was confident he could handle the two of them.

FOURTEEN

Sandoval crept toward the cave entrance in Nightwind Canyon. He was gambling that the wind direction would prevent the horses or mules from catching his scent or sound and raising an alarm.

Cat-footing to the very mouth of the cave, he paused to look and listen. Faint, ragged snoring reached his ears. No light from lantern or torch, but he did catch a whiff of wood smoke. If anyone was on guard, he was inside. Where were their horses? Evidently they felt secure in their assumed isolation. He resisted a foolhardy impulse to rush inside, gun blazing. Even with darkness and surprise on his side, a rescue attempt was too risky. He'd wait for a better chance.

Instead, he completed his silent task and faded away toward Lodestar. Familiar with every boulder and gully in the area, he jogged with swift confidence down the rugged canyon.

The wind was sounding the bell in the tower of San Juan Church. He liked to think it was the ringing of the Angelus at six in the morning, but it was not yet six. He missed hearing the Angelus rung at six in the morning, at noon, and again at six in the evening. The wind rang the bell when it wished, and it was not the pattern he'd grown up with—three sets of three taps each, then a full minute of loud continuous ringing. But, in his solitude before anyone came to Lodestar, he often found himself pausing to say the traditional prayer when the bell rang, "*El Angel del Señor anuncio a Maria. Y concibio por obra del Espiritu Santo. Dios te salve, Maria. Llena eres de gracia . . .*" The angel of the Lord declared unto Mary and she conceived of the Holy Spirit. Hail Mary, full of grace, the Lord is with thee . . . Old habits died hard.

An hour later he climbed the outside stairs to the second floor of the old hotel and felt his way to a room along the hall. Striking a match, he located a broken chair and dragged it to a south-facing back window. As soon as he sat down to await daylight, weariness nearly overcame him. He'd slept little since first finding Charvein unconscious on the edge of town. How long ago was that? One day? Two? The hours seemed to run together in a continuous stream, broken only by a quick nap here and there. He stared, unseeing, through the window into the blackness.

He'd been here four years now and recalled being lonely only once or twice. Mostly, his loyal animals—God's innocent creatures—were enough companionship for him. Lodestar's formidable isolation was the reason he'd taken up his hermitage here. Now the town was awash in strangers, and he was being forced to deal with them by accommodating himself to the pace of a world he'd left behind.

In spite of his confident words to Lucy, a heavy lump of dread lay in his stomach. He suspected Charvein had died of his wounds. Normally, he was optimistic and didn't worry about things he couldn't control, accepting whatever happened without question. Perhaps Lucy's anxiety was affecting him. He'd wait to see who emerged from the canyon in the morning.

The wind gusted with increased fury, shaking Lodestar like a terrier shaking a rat. Above the creaking wooden beams, banging shutters, rattling tin cans, he heard the familiar mellow tones of his personal wind chime—the heavy clapper lightly tolling the bell in the church belfry. He smiled. He'd come to regard himself as Lodestar's mayor, banker, saloonkeeper, merchant, guardian, and caretaker. All things that happened here were his business and his concern.

Leaning forward on the windowsill, he rested his head on his folded forearms. Slipping into a doze, he felt relaxed for the first time since he could remember. All this turmoil had benefited him in one way—it had driven from his mind the crushing mental anguish he carried every day.

He slept. It was a light sleep, with his subconscious alert—not a condition guaranteed to allow complete rest. But it sufficed—and kept him safe.

Sometime later, the lessening of the wind and clatter outside brought back his consciousness. He raised his head and carefully wiped away the gummy residue matting his eyelids. Squinting through a cracked pane, he noted the coming of daylight in the light brown haze.

Something moved. He blinked and tried to focus on the distant speck, wishing he had a pair of field glasses. For a long minute he watched the moving figure approaching from the distant mouth of Nightwind Canyon. It wasn't a wolf, coyote, burro, or cat. It was upright—a lone man. Sandoval slid his rifle over the sill and lined up the buckhorn sight with the front bead on the end of the barrel.

Charvein saw the first rays of the rising sun glint off something in a window of the hotel. A pane of glass? A gun barrel? Forgetting his fatigue, he dashed behind a nearby boulder. Pistol in hand, he watched for several seconds. Whatever it was disappeared. It had been there and then was gone. Probably nothing to worry about. He cautiously continued on toward the back of the row of buildings.

Less than three hundred yards away, he saw a man come around a building, loping toward him, waving. He stopped and squinted in the morning sun. Sandoval! Relief flooded over him.

Two minutes later the men met.

"By God, am I glad to see a friendly face!" Charvein said, gripping his friend by the shoulders.

"What happened? You're not hurt?"

"Let's get out of the open," Charvein said, taking his arm and hurrying around the hotel. "I expect the two of them will be after me shortly."

"Two?"

Charvein briefly summed up the events of the night. "I'll take the woman and get out of town. Can I borrow your mule, or your burro?"

"Yes. Let's go," Sandoval said, obviously relieved. "What about those two? And where has Boyd gone?"

"Can't answer the last question. I reckon he's hightailed it back to Carson or Virginia City. If he took their horses, we're stuck with those no-goods."

Sandoval gripped his rifle and stared back toward Nightwind Canyon.

"Don't worry. I won't leave until we take care of them, one way or another," Charvein assured him.

"How much of a head start do you have on them?"

Charvein shrugged. "They were still passed out drunk when Boyd and I took off our separate ways. They're likely hungover and hopping mad right now. Fact is, they could be right on my tail this minute."

"Your head okay?" Sandoval asked, pointing at the blood on Charvein's shirt collar.

"Think so. Still have a headache from busting that boulder with my head." He attempted a grin. "They said they heard my shot at the snake and came to investigate."

Sandoval nodded. "That's where I spotted them—picking you up and loading you on that mule. Followed to see where they took you."

The men rounded the corner of the hotel to the boardwalk in front.

"Lucy is alone," Sandoval said. "I told her I'd be back at least by daylight. We'd best go now or she might come looking for us and get herself in trouble." He stepped off the boardwalk into the street—and stopped dead. "Damn!"

A horse with an empty saddle snorted and plunged away from them, tossing its head. "That one of their horses?"

Charvein looked at the spooked sorrel, dragging its reins in the dust. "Nope. Never saw that animal before."

The two men looked blankly at each other.

The saddled gelding stopped thirty yards away and turned to face them. A torn shirt hung from one side of his bridle.

"Someone on the playa," Sandoval said. "The sun and dust have claimed another victim."

"Let's see if we can round him up," Charvein said. "We need a good mount."

"Where's your canteen?"

"Still in the cave. I didn't stop to take it when Boyd cut me loose."

"That horse must be thirsty." Sandoval eased the canteen strap over his head. "I have a half gallon in here. Pull that rusty pan out of the trash pile over there. We'll lure him with a drink."

Moving slowly, the men brought the pan into the middle

of the street, and Sandoval, splashing loudly, poured most of the contents of his canteen into it. Then they backed away several paces.

The horse came forward a few steps, nostrils quivering, eager yet wary. Charvein moved out of the animal's peripheral vision as the sorrel lowered its head and began to drink. The two quarts was only a good taste; Charvein would have to be quick.

While the horse watched Sandoval, Charvein eased closer until the horse sensed his presence and jerked his head up with a snort. But he was too late. Charvein leapt and grabbed the saddle horn. The horse plunged, lifting him off the ground, but when the horse came down, Charvein sprang up and threw a leg over the saddle. The startled horse bowed his back and bucked twice, three times, then whirled, trying to rid himself of this terrifying thing. But then he crow-hopped, stiff-legged, several times and stopped, obviously fatigued. He'd been startled, but he had been broken to the saddle by someone and so submitted to the rider on his back.

Charvein reached down and retrieved the dragging reins, yanked the torn shirt loose from the bridle, then walked the animal over to a sagging hitching rail where Sandoval tied him securely. "Check the saddlebags. Might find out who he belongs to."

"Nothing but jerky, a razor, spare socks, and a plug of chewing tobacco. Some other odds and ends, but no name on anything—not even on this shirt."

"Ever seen a saddle like this?" Charvein asked.

"*Sí*. It's old." He stroked the worn leather. "A stock saddle used by vaqueros in California about 1850. Long, slim saddle horn, deep seat, tapaderos."

"No conchos or fancy silver work," Charvein noted.

"No. This is a working saddle. Very comfortable. A man could sit one of these for many hours. It has seen much use."

"What do you think happened to the man who rode this?" Charvein asked, dismounting and stroking the horse's nose.

Sandoval squinted at the brightening sky. "Probably not far away," he said, pointing. A dozen black vultures wheeled in a lazy, descending vortex less than a mile distant.

"But for the grace of God . . . ," Charvein murmured. "Shall we go to his aid?"

"He has no more problems in this world," Sandoval said, making the sign of the cross. "But we do."

Charvein followed his gaze to the lower end of the street. Stepenaw and Weasel. The big man raised a long rifle.

"Get down!" Charvein grabbed Sandoval's arm and pulled him back under the roofed boardwalk.

The boom of Boyd's .50-caliber Sharps blasted the stillness, and a lead slug shivered a window two feet to their left.

The startled horse jerked back, but the reins held him fast to the rail.

Stepenaw lumbered toward them, apparently unafraid of return fire. Weasel followed at an awkward run, firing a Colt with his good hand.

Charvein kicked open a nearby door. "Inside!" he yelled, squeezing off two shots at the men who were out of effective pistol range.

Stepenaw paused, yanked down the lever to open the breech, shoved in another long cartridge, and slammed it home.

Sandoval scrambled inside the room and took up a kneeling position with his rifle at the broken window.

Charvein threw two more shots in the outlaws' general direction, then dove for cover as the Sharps boomed again.

When Charvein looked up, he saw that the pair had dodged inside a saloon diagonally across the street. The octagonal barrel of the buffalo gun protruded from the edge of the saloon doorway. They were still sixty to seventy yards away.

Charvein's ears rang for several seconds after the last exchange of shots.

Finally, Stepenaw yelled, "Hey, mister, you and Boyd might as well come on outta there. I got the big gun now and it'll shoot right through that wall."

"He thinks you're Boyd," Charvein muttered, surprised. "They don't know anyone else is in town. He figures Boyd and I left together."

"Where's your wounded buddy?" Charvein yelled back. "I want to give him a matching bullet."

"Likely slipping around to put a slug in your back!" Stepenaw crowed. "He's got a mighty grudge to settle with you."

Another few seconds of silence.

"Why don't we call a truce and parlay?" Sandoval suggested, quietly. "Let 'em know I'm not Boyd."

"That your horse, mister?" Stepenaw called.

"Yeah. You want him? I'll sell him to you."

"Then you was lyin' about your horse being shot out from under you."

"I just found this horse running loose, but he's for sale," Charvein yelled back. Then, under his breath to Sandoval he said, "He might be trying to keep us busy talking so Weasel can sneak up on us. I don't see any sign of him." He glanced around at the interior of the old dry goods store. The wooden counter blocked his view of the back door.

Sandoval shoved his rifle barrel through the broken window and fired off a shot, cocked and fired, and then a third time. The echoes of the blasts faded down the empty street and were swallowed up in the vast stillness.

Picking up his cue, Charvein yelled, "We got a little firepower, too!"

After a pause, "This ain't getting' us nowhere!" came Stepenaw's shout from across the street. "We need to know where the rest of the gold is, so's me and Weasel can get our share. That's all we want. Then we'll head outta here and leave you be."

"Did he just say the *rest* of the gold?" He looked at Sandoval. "They musta found some of it."

"Let's call a truce and sort this out." Sandoval glanced up and down the empty street, then toward the back room of the store, as if Weasel might be sneaking in to ambush them.

"I'm game," Charvein said, handing over the white shirt he'd retrieved from the horse's bridle. Sandoval tied it by the sleeves to his rifle barrel, thrust it out the window, and waved it back and forth.

"Flag of truce!" Charvein shouted through cupped hands. "Want to come out and talk."

A short silence, then, "All right. No guns. Meet in the middle of the street."

"Call Weasel out where we can see him," Charvein added.

The wounded man apparently heard them, and he stepped out from between the barbershop and the bakery directly across the street.

Could these two be trusted to come unarmed? Did either of them have a hideout gun? Charvein was more concerned about Weasel than Stepenaw. They'd have to chance it, since this Mexican standoff could last the rest of the day. Charvein and Sandoval had no water or food and were not equipped for a protracted siege. Not only that, but Lucy could hear the gunfire and might take it into her head to seek them out.

"Okay, come ahead and we'll do the same," Stepenaw yelled. "Leave your guns and show your hands."

Charvein unbuckled his gunbelt and set it on the floor. Sandoval propped his rifle against the wall.

The four men advanced into the sunlight and approached one another in the dusty street. The wind had died.

The pair of escapees looked even rougher than they had the previous night, showing puffy, bloodshot eyes, unshaven jowls, matted hair. Weasel looked peaked and was grimly silent. He held his wounded arm with his free hand, cradling it in his makeshift sling.

"Who the hell are you?" Weasel demanded, staring at Sandoval. "And where's Boyd?"

"Reckon he took off," Charvein said. "And, from the looks of things, he took your horses, too."

"You ain't answered my question," Weasel said, staring at Sandoval.

"*No comprende*," Sandoval replied with a shrug. "I am Carlos Vasquez. I come to this town to work an old claim. I ran into this hombre who said he needed my help to return to Virginia City." He affected a heavier Hispanic accent than normal.

"That your horse, yonder?" Stepenaw asked.

"*Sí.*"

"Figured it belonged to a breed, from the looks of the saddle," Stepenaw said, nodding at his deduction.

Charvein looked sideways at Sandoval, who retained a poker face.

"Which way did Boyd go?" Weasel asked. "We got business with him."

"After he cut me loose, he disappeared into that dust storm in the dark. I didn't ask no questions; I just lit a shuck."

"Well he dropped this on his way out," Stepenaw said, patting the side pocket of his jacket. "I don't have no gun," he added, sliding a hand in his pocket and pulling out a small gold bar. "Reckon that SOB was lying all along about not finding the gold. He got us drunk, then slid out, but dropped one of the bars in the dark."

Charvein was stunned. "You think he had the bars stashed in his saddlebags in the cave last night."

"Dunno. 'Tain't likely, since the damned stuff weighs over a hundred pounds. Besides, we searched his saddlebags when we first jumped him the other day. All I know is this is one of the gold bars we took offen that train five years ago. See this mark? That's what was showed at our trial and got us sent to the pen."

Charvein had serious doubts about where the bar had come from, but he chose not to voice them. "Where'd you say you found that?"

"Right outside the entrance to the cave."

Charvein nodded.

"We ain't got time to palaver," the big man said. "You, breed . . . we'll shave some slivers offen this bar and buy that horse from you."

"I'm not sure he is for sale, señor."

"I ain't askin' you; I'm telling you."

"You are not armed, señor."

"I could bust you in two with one hand. I don't need a gun," Stepenaw growled. "But we ain't got time for all that. Boyd's gettin' away with the rest of the stash while we're talkin'. Here, Mex, take some o' this gold. It's more good metal than you're likely to find combing through the tailings around these old mines."

Charvein gave a quiet nod.

"*Bueno, señor.* I accept your offer. But my horse, he is very tired. He cannot carry two of you."

"No matter. We'll take turns. He been fed and watered lately?"

Sandoval shook his head. "No, señor."

"Shit. Well, we have to climb that hill for more water anyway, afore we start out. We'll find some forage along the way." Stepenaw looked glum. "Boyd took off with the gold and all the animals—his own two mules, our two horses"—he counted on his fingers—"and the horse that woman was riding. He'll have a fresh mount all the way to Virginia City."

"We'll never catch up to him," Weasel whined.

"Would you rather sit around here and starve while he hightails it?" Stepenaw asked. "Ain't the gold why we come here? Why we busted out? You wanta let him get clean away? He's likely laughing his ass off right now."

Anger brought the color back into Weasel's face. He eased his arm out of the sling, unwrapped the crude bandage, and looked at the swollen, angry wound.

Charvein cringed at the sight of the red streaks radiating up the forearm.

"Damn the gold! I gotta find a regular sawbones to tend this arm. It's begun to mortify."

"All the more reason to get outta here and head for Virginia City. That's likely where Boyd's goin'. If we can't catch up to him across the playa, we'll find him in town," Stepenaw said. "We'll get him, the gold, and have your arm treated." While he spoke, he'd taken out his clasp knife and was whittling off gold shavings. After a minute, he hefted the pile of shavings in his hand. "Here ya go. About three ounces there, I'd judge." He continued scraping more small pieces and added them to the pile. "Make it four. That's roughly sixty dollars." He reached out and dropped the gold into Sandoval's extended hand.

"Treat him with kindness, señor," Sandoval quavered in an old man's voice, looking at the tired horse.

"We can't go to Virginia City," Weasel said. "Boyd is a free man. But we're wanted by the law. I ain't about to land back behind those walls. I'll die first."

"You might croak anyway, without you get that arm fixed," Stepenaw said bluntly.

"Let's go," Weasel said, turning away.

Stepenaw backed up, continuing to face them. "We still under a flag of truce?"

Charvein nodded.

"You won't shoot at us while we're leaving town?"

"We'll hold our fire if you hold yours," Charvein said.

The big man moved warily around them toward the horse still tied at the hitching rail. Jerking the reins loose, he led the sorrel away and joined Weasel, who had retrieved his gunbelt, and handed Stepenaw the big Sharps.

"Thank God they're leaving," Sandoval breathed as the pair disappeared into a side street toward their water source on the hill beyond. "Let's get our guns. As soon as they're gone, you can take Lucy and my mule and burro and start for Virginia City."

"Virginia City, hell!" Charvein muttered. "Thought I'd hit a dead end and was about to give up. But now that I know Boyd has the gold, I'm back on his trail."

"What?" Sandoval's eyes went wide.

"I was hired to do a job, and it won't be done until I find out where Boyd is going with that stash of gold bars."

FIFTEEN

"Let me come with you," Lucy pled. "I can ride the burro. I won't be any trouble."

Charvein continued with his preparations, dragging the double-rigged saddle to the center of the cavern, piling three full canteens next to it. "Lucy, I was planning to take you straight back to Virginia City, but I'll have to put that off a few days. Boyd has about a six-hour head start on me as it is. And he's trailing fresh mounts. I'll be lucky to catch him. This might turn into a long chase. And I won't expose you to that."

"Not much chance you'll overtake him this side of Carson or Virginia City," Sandoval commented.

"He's not likely to head for town just yet—not packing all that stolen gold. But as long as the wind doesn't wipe out his tracks, I can trail him wherever he goes. I'm not carrying extra weight or trailing extra horses that I'll have to find provender for."

Sandoval looked doubtful. "If he left a couple hours before daylight, the wind has probably scoured away most of his tracks." He shrugged. "But, if it's any help, we're due for a change. Those winds aren't usually ripsnorters more than three days in a row. And there'll be a three-quarter moon tonight."

Charvein added a twenty-pound sack of oats and a nose bag to his pile. "You'll be safer here," he told Lucy. "And I can travel faster alone. I'll be back for you."

"When?" She looked doleful.

"Not sure. Depends on Boyd, mostly. He's strong and resourceful. He's determined to keep that gold at any cost. And he's armed with my rifle and his Colt. I'll need some grit and some luck to get him."

"You said you didn't have to arrest him—only discover where the gold is and report to your boss," Sandoval said, stuffing small sacks of beans and coffee into the saddlebags.

"True enough. If I can get close enough to catch sight of him, I'll hang back. That's what I was trying to do on the way out here. And you know how that turned out. Wish I could somehow make myself invisible. But, 'If wishes were horses, beggars would ride.'"

"What?"

"Old expression my father used."

Sandoval looked thoughtful. "If I were the one packing a hundred twenty pounds of gold bars, I'd sure be in a hurry to find another safe place to stash it. You just can't go among men in towns with that much gold—especially stolen gold—on the back of a horse or mule. Somebody's going to find out about it for sure. Then your life won't be worth a sliver of that gold Stepenaw gave me."

"If I had any money, I'd buy your mule and rig from you."

"It's yours on loan only," Sandoval replied. "That way I know you'll be back."

"The only way I won't keep my word is if I'm dead." He heaved the saddle to his shoulder and started toward the mule picketed just outside the cavern entrance. Sandoval's quick, sure hands were there to help.

"How long should I wait before I can assume you're not coming back?" Lucy asked.

"You'll know." Then he paused to look at her tear-streaked face, her disheveled dark hair hanging down, the dark shadows under her eyes. He calculated time and distance in his head. "Give me at least a few days—no more than ten."

"Life was uncertain in medieval times," she said, almost to herself. "And it's uncertain now. In Walter Scott's novels the hero always lives, and the maiden is always rescued and lives happily ever after." She smiled ruefully. "Real life is not like those novels."

Charvein felt suddenly sorry for her—an innocent, naïve woman caught up in a brutal kidnapping, then subjected to treatment her previous life had ill-equipped her for. "Well," he said gently, walking over and taking her hand, "we've already had two rescues—one of you and one of me. Now all that remains is for me to track this robber and the gold, then come back here to take you home." He smiled and pulled her close in a reassuring hug. "Then it's up to you to live happily ever after." He could feel her heartbeat quicken as he held her close.

He stepped back, taking satisfaction in the new glow of hope on her face.

He snatched the reins of the mule loose from a big mesquite bush and mounted.

"Remember, Stepenaw and Weasel are also on Boyd's trail," Sandoval cautioned. "Neither of them will hesitate to gun you down. And the big man has that long rifle."

"The stars aren't aligned for me to die."

"Wish you'd change your mind and take this young lady back to Carson City. She can have this burro with my blessing."

"Later. I'm burning daylight. Keep her safe till I get back." The mule trotted quickly down the slope out into the open.

There was no need for caution now that everyone else was gone from Lodestar. Charvein rode down Center Street and out onto the playa, feeling better than he had for some time. His head still ached dully, but he was fed and carried plenty of water for himself and his stout mule, who was well rested and ready for work.

The sun lacked three hours of noon, but its midsummer rays burned through the back of his thin cotton shirt. He'd lost his own hat but had borrowed an old felt from Sandoval. He thought of the man who'd become his close friend and confidant. Whenever all this was finished, he vowed to find out more about Sandoval than just his name. He claimed to be mostly Incan—and looked it. What had he done, where had he been, before taking up lodging as Lodestar's only resident?

As Charvein had feared, last night's wind had blown away, or filled in, all tracks on the soil of the ancient dry lake bed. All, that is, except the most recent, made since daylight—the hoofprints of the stray horse. A separate set of boot prints showed Stepenaw, the heavier of the two, walking. The trail led west, in the general direction of Carson City or Virginia City. The two men were probably more than an hour ahead of him, roughly four miles or so, he estimated. He squinted ahead across the glare of the dun-colored playa. No sign of them. Lost somewhere in the shimmering mirage. His mule trotted steadily; he'd probably catch the slow-moving pair by early afternoon.

Charvein scanned the terrain for even the slightest signs of several horses that might indicate where Boyd had gone. Drawing the mule to a walk, he searched the ground carefully. He wondered if Boyd would have risked his own life and the lives of his horses and mules by starting out in that dust storm. Boyd was armed and well mounted and had nothing to fear, except the forces of nature. He wouldn't even have been able to hold a direction in that darkness and blowing dust. Would've made more sense for him to hole up in a protected barn to await the coming of light and calmer weather. But nothing about Boyd's action seemed to make sense. It was possible he'd not gone west from Lodestar at all. Perhaps he was headed south or east, or north. But there was nothing in those directions for many miles— no human habitation and very likely no water this time of year, even in the low desert mountains. No. In all likelihood, his route was westerly.

As Charvein rode across the empty playa, puffs of dust rising from the mule's plodding hooves, he began to wonder if his zeal had carried him on a fruitless chase.

He caught movement out of the corner of his eye: the circling vultures he'd seen earlier, but now more—perhaps twenty—wheeled against the brassy sky. If something was already dead out there, why hadn't they landed and begun their quarreling feast? Maybe too many of their kin were already at table and no room for the rest. Charvein wished he knew more about the habits of these scavengers. But buzzards and vultures had always repulsed him, and he ignored them when he could.

On impulse, he reined his mule away from the tracks he was following. Might as well see what the birds were after. Probably a coyote or some other small animal that had given up a harsh existence.

Distance over the flat, featureless surface was deceiving, and it was an hour before he arrived. He found a saddled horse, standing with its head drooping. Charvein guided his mule close, and the animal didn't react or move away. Dried blood caked his left flank and rump. A half dozen big vultures were on the ground several yards away, awaiting their chance. They began to move, and two of them flapped away at Charvein's approach.

He dismounted and poured water into his hat for the animal to drink. The horse sucked it empty and nuzzled him for more. Charvein poured him another quart. That was enough for now. But it seemed to revive the horse.

He mounted the mule, trailed the horse by its reins, and started again. He'd gone no more than a hundred yards when his stomach contracted at the sight of a man lying partially covered in dust. He reined up and dismounted again, ground reining the mule and tying the horse's reins to the saddle horn.

The prone figure moved slightly, and Charvein knelt quickly at his side, uncorking one of the canteens. He supported the man's head and dribbled water over the parched lips. At first, there was no reaction, but then he began to swallow, and Charvein was careful not to let him choke. The big man's shirt was caked with dried blood from at least two wounds. It was apparent he had lost a lot of blood. Charvein leaned over to shade the man's face. He blinked and appeared to focus. Charvein tipped up the canteen again. "Easy, now. Not too much." Was he too far gone to hear, or understand? "What happened? Can you tell me who did this?"

He attempted to reply, but nothing came out. Licking his lips, he tried again. "Rankin," he whispered hoarsely. Charvein had to lean close to catch his words. "Buck Rankin," he said.

"Rankin?" Charvein had known a Buck Rankin when they were both lawmen—Buck, a deputy marshal, and Charvein, a railroad detective.

Charvein rocked back on his heels, his mind in a whirl. Buck Rankin shot this man? Then this wounded man must be a fugitive.

"Where is Rankin?"

The man was fading. "Posse," he whispered.

Rankin had retired years ago. Had he volunteered to lead a posse?

"Where is this posse?" Charvein asked urgently. Surely Rankin wouldn't have shot a man and left him to die out here—unless Rankin was also wounded and had gone off for help—or to die himself. What the hell had happened here?

Charvein gave him another drink. After two swallows, the man coughed and a bloody froth came to his lips. He gasped, took two or three long breaths, as if clinging to life, then went limp. Charvein checked his throat for a pulse. Nothing. He eased the man's head to the ground.

He sighed and stood up. A man dead on the playa at the hand of Buck Rankin. Maybe it was a long-range gun battle, or the horse wouldn't be wounded. Buck Rankin was too good a shot for that.

He walked over to the docile animal and gave him another drink out of the soggy felt hat. He noted the saddle carried no saddlebags, no rifle scabbard, no canteen. Had Buck taken them? Or had this man fled from somewhere and left them behind? He checked the holstered Colt. It was fully loaded. No burned powder residue on the face of the cylinder, and it smelled of gun oil. It had been cleaned since last fired. That compounded the mystery. Buck Rankin would never shoot a man multiple times from ambush.

Charvein stooped and muscled the man's heavy body up onto his shoulder, draped it across the saddle, tied the hands and feet together under the belly, then ran a loop of the lariat from the man's belt to the saddle horn.

After this exertion in the heat, he paused for a drink and to wipe the sweat from his face. He put on his wet, cool hat and looked around. Now what? The weathered buildings of

Lodestar were barely visible to the east. He began to have second thoughts about his pursuit of Boyd. It'd be a different matter if there were a clear trail to follow. But Boyd's direction was only a guess, although Stepenaw and Weasel were betting on Virginia City and were headed there themselves. Now Charvein had a nagging doubt. If this dead man's horse stayed close while his owner lived, then whose horse had he and Sandoval found running loose in Lodestar this morning? Was there another dead man out here somewhere—Buck Rankin perhaps?

The heat of midday was growing intense. He'd bury this body on the spot had he brought anything to dig with. Hauling the big man across the playa to God knew where didn't make sense. Yet Charvein couldn't just leave him to the vultures. Outlaw or not, he deserved better than that.

Charvein decided to ride another hour to the west in a wide circle to see if he could cut Boyd's trail. It would be easily recognizable because there were five animals. If he found nothing, he'd return to Lodestar and see if Sandoval knew this man. They could bury him in the long unused town graveyard.

The sun slid past meridian, and Charvein pulled down his hat brim against its rays. He again regretted the loss of his field glasses. Those twin lenses would have extended his vision a long way, eliminating the need for so much useless riding. But he had to deal with what was, not what he wished for.

After a monotonous hour, he began to doze in the heat, swaying in the saddle. He jerked upright and scanned the sand- and salt-streaked playa. Nothing. He dismounted and scooped some oats from the sack into the nose bag and put it on his mule. He fed the horse a double handful of grain from his hat. When they'd finished, he watered both animals from the hat.

It was then he confirmed his decision to return to Lodestar; he didn't have enough water for himself and both animals to go another day. As cunning as Boyd was, he would likely head for the desert mountains first to hide the gold in one of the thousands of canyons or caves.

Charvein put on his hat and remounted. A large, black spot caught his attention. It was some distance off, wavering in the dancing water mirage. Before turning back, he would investigate. Probably nothing more than some lava rocks, or a dark clump of shrubs.

Within a few minutes, he picked up the clear trail of three horses, all heading in the same direction. His heart rate quickened, thinking at first he'd cut Boyd's trail. But then, he knew his quarry had five animals—not three. And four of them would be trailed, one behind the other, so the tracks would be atop one another. These were spread out abreast and were cut deeper into the soft soil, as if the horses carried the weight of riders. These tracks had been made since the wind had ceased this morning. Charvein urged his mule to a trot to catch up, hoping the bouncing would not jar the body off the led horse.

In twenty minutes the black blob had grown and split into three. Charvein slowed his mule to a walk to save his strength and wind. As he did so, he realized the three dark figures were three riders approaching at a gallop. They rapidly closed the gap. He drew rein and stopped, reaching for his Colt. What was he riding into? It wouldn't be the first time curiosity had imperiled him. If these three riders proved to be hostile, there was nothing he could do about it now. The three had spread several yards apart and would shortly have him boxed in. Even if he turned to flee, his tired mule wasn't fast enough to outrun them. Sun glinted on rifle barrels. He breathed deeply and steeled himself to await the outcome.

The riders slowed as they approached, each man carrying a long gun across his saddle. Wide hats hid their faces in shadow. They reined up within talking distance, one man wide to each side and one facing him. The spokesman in front said, "Holster that shooter." He raised his rifle a few inches for emphasis.

Charvein complied. Without turning his head, he saw the other two bring their rifles to bear. The three were rough-looking characters—unshaven and dirty, apparently on the trail for some days.

The leader jabbed his rifle toward the led horse. "That's Schooner Douglas's hoss."

"Found him back there, wounded," Charvein said, his own voice sounding oddly rough and strained.

The rider to his left dismounted and came forward on foot.

"Just set easy, mister," the man in front said.

Charvein glanced at the walker, who bent down to get a look at the face of the man tied across the saddle. "It's Schooner, all right," the man said, retreating to his own horse.

"I found him back there on the playa, near dead. Gave him a little water, but he was too far gone. Lung shot, I'd guess. He died in a few minutes."

"A damned lie," the leader growled. "You and your pardner likely gunned him down when he and Rankin came after you. Where is your little pardner, anyway? You two split up? Well, I reckon one's better than none. Maybe the reward'll be just as good for one jailbird as two—especially since we're saving the state the expense of trying and hanging a murderer."

Charvein caught his breath as three rounds were racheted into the chambers of three Winchesters, and the men brought the weapons to their shoulders.

SIXTEEN

"Wait!" Charvein raised his hands, still clutching both sets of reins. "I didn't kill him!" he shouted, staring at each man in turn. He didn't think any of them would shoot him while their gazes were locked. "If I shot him, why would I be hauling his body with me?" He held his breath, expecting to feel three rifle bullets slam into his chest. Sweat trickled down his sides under his shirt. He didn't dare move.

"Hold up, boys. Let's hear him out," the leader said. "Climb down off that mule, mister."

Charvein dismounted, ground reining the animals.

The three men remained in their saddles.

"Where'd you find him?"

"Two miles back. He was only able to say a couple words before he died."

"I'll bet!" the rider to his right said, spitting his derision into the dust. "Can't you see he's makin' it up as he goes? Tryin' to think of a quick alibi to keep us from carrying out a proper execution right now."

The leader in front held up his hand for silence. "Give him his say. Once we shoot him, he's a long time dead."

Charvein looked closer at the man's round face under the hat brim. A coating of brown stubble made him look older than he likely was. The wire-rimmed glasses suggested a land office clerk or salesman. But there was no mistaking the look of determination.

"I left Lodestar this morning headed for Virginia City," Charvein said, more to break the tension than anything else.

"We'll get to you later. Tell us about Douglas."

Charvein sucked in the heated air, glad to still be breathing. He'd try to stretch this brief reprieve. "The buzzards led me to him. Found this wounded horse. He was lying nearly dead nearby. He'd lost a lot of blood." He paused and took another deep breath.

"Quit stalling. What did he say?"

"I gave him water and asked who shot him. He whispered, 'Brackin,' or something like that. Could hardly hear him, so I asked again. This time I was sure he said, 'Buck Rankin.'" Charvein didn't indicate he knew Rankin.

A significant look passed among the three men.

"Go on," the leader said.

"He was able to say only one more word—'posse.' Then he died. That's all I can tell you. No saddlebags to look through, so I had no idea who he was." He shook his head. "Didn't know what to make of that. But I didn't have a shovel to bury him, and I wasn't about to leave him for the buzzards. Thought I'd take his body to Virginia City."

The leader gazed at him silently for a moment. "What's your name and where you from?"

"Marc Charvein. Virginia City."

"Your name sounds familiar.

"I was a railroad detective a few years back."

"What's your business out here?"

"I might ask you the same."

"You forget who's holding the guns here. Answer the question."

"I was deputized to find a man."

"Who?"

"Denson Boyd."

"Boyd . . . Boyd? Didn't I see in the paper where he was recently released from prison?"

"Right. The governor pardoned him."

"He's already a wanted man?"

Charvein wasn't sure how much he should reveal. For all he knew, they could be trying to get their hands on the gold bullion as well. Without answering the question, he said, "You boys after somebody, too?"

"We're the posse."

Charvein jerked his head toward the dead man. "The one he mentioned?"

"The same. He was one of us. Lemme see your papers or your badge."

"In my pocket."

The man nodded, and Charvein slowly put a hand into his vest pocket, withdrawing the worn silver star he'd been issued. He stepped forward and handed it up for inspection. The man grunted and handed it back. "I reckon we're all on the same side. I believe what you're telling us, Charvein. What I can't figure out is why Rankin did it." He dismounted and stuck out his hand. "Name's Jude Belcher. This here's Tommy Conway and Bill Owens."

The two sheathed their carbines and dismounted, apparently glad to stretch their legs.

"Who's Buck Rankin?" Charvein asked.

"He's a retired marshal and was leading this posse, trailing Boyd's two ex-partners who busted outta prison in Carson and kidnapped a girl." He stepped to the horse Charvein led and lifted the dead man's head by the hair. "Um . . . He was a tough one. Never figured him to get gunned down." He looked up at Charvein. "Rankin and Douglas musta got into it." He paused. "Rankin didn't think much of us as a posse. My gut feeling is that he wanted the reward money for himself. Sometime in the middle o' all that wind and dust last night, he and Douglas took off. Dunno what happened or why. The way Rankin'd been talking, I figure one or both of them were leaving us to make do on our own while they went after the convicts." He returned to his horse and helped himself to a drink from his canteen. "You didn't see nothing of another man, did you?"

"Nope." Charvein didn't mention finding the loose horse in Lodestar, but now he suspected it belonged to the missing Rankin.

"Reckon you didn't catch up with Boyd."

"Tracked him to Lodestar, but he got away from me. Don't know where he went. I was just on my way home."

"What'd you say he did?"

"I didn't. Just trying to snag him retrieving that gold he stole five years ago. It was never recovered, and the owner wants it back."

"Well, we got something in common, then, since we're after his two ex-partners." His face brightened. "You don't reckon they're all after that stolen gold?"

Charvein shrugged.

"We'll bury poor Schooner here on the playa and then you can come with us back to Lodestar."

"Waste of time," Charvein said. "I just come from there and the town's empty."

"Hmmm."

"But I recollect something that might be of use to you."

"What's that?"

"Before I got sidetracked by those buzzards, I was traveling along the trail of a horse and a man afoot leading west toward Washoe. Reckon that might be your two fugitives?"

"Could be." Belcher gave him a dubious look. "Mighty convenient of you to think of that."

"I was more concerned with keeping you boys from ventilating my hide. The business end of three Winchesters affected my memory."

"Where is this trail?"

Charvein glanced at the sun and then back the way he'd come, to orient himself. He pointed to the right. "Just go straight north. You should cut it in less than a mile unless they changed direction."

Belcher swung into the saddle. "Come along and show us." He failed to keep the distrust out of his voice.

"I wasn't really going that direction."

"Won't be much outta your way."

"What about him?" Charvein jerked a thumb toward the body.

"Schooner will keep a little longer." Belcher wheeled his horse around, followed by Owens and Conway. "When we cut the trail you mentioned, we can stop and bury him. We're packin' a short shovel and our belt knives. We can bust through this soft crust."

Charvein could see he had no choice. Thrusting a foot into the stirrup, he swung aboard the mule, took up the reins of both animals, and led the way north. The other three fell in beside and slightly behind him, spreading out to avoid the disturbed dust.

They rode in silence, Charvein hoping the two escapees hadn't stopped or veered off course. If he didn't find the track, he was in trouble.

But, luckily, the track was there, just where he'd guessed

they'd find it, only now it showed two men afoot and one horse. Rankin's horse must have been further gone than he realized, or the two convicts were just saving him.

"There it is." He pointed at the fresh trail.

The three men dismounted for a closer look, apparently eager to see the first real signs of their elusive quarry.

"Pair of big boots and some smaller ones," Conway said. "Fits the sheriff's description of Stepenaw and Savage."

"But why're they headed west toward Virginia City or Carson?" Belcher mused, half-aloud. "That's where they come from. And why only one horse? Where's the woman?"

"Yeah. We were told they got away with three horses, the woman hostage riding one of them," Owens said.

"Hell, you know how we were pounded by those dust storms," Belcher said. "They likely lost two of the horses and have the woman riding this one remaining animal. Betcha they're in bad need of food and water, or they'd be trying to hide their trail."

"Could be anything," Owens said, taking off his hat and mopping his bald head with a blue bandanna.

"Okay, boys, let's get poor Schooner underground. These tracks are fresh. With the two of them walking, it won't take us long to catch them."

Charvein pitched in with his sheath knife to help scrape out a grave for Douglas. Owens took the short shovel and made the dirt fly. Under the cracked crust, the earth was soft for two feet down before he reached solid subsoil. Then he turned the shovel over to Belcher, and in another ten minutes, they'd cut a hole three feet deep and were ready to quit.

Conway pulled the rolled blanket off the dead man's horse while Charvein untied the body and retrieved his lariat. They shortly had the big man wrapped and in the ground.

"No rocks around to keep off wolves and coyotes," Belcher panted, stamping down the dirt. "That's the best we can do."

"Reckon we ought to say a prayer, or something?" Conway asked.

"Schooner was a hard drinker and a hard man. Reckon he's the Lord's or the Devil's now," Belcher replied.

"You ain't supposed to speak ill of the dead, no matter what they done in life," Owens said. "Lemme think . . . He gave me a free drink once. And I hear tell he was kind to whores down on their luck."

"Not much of a recommendation, but I reckon it'll have to do," Belcher said. "Let's get going." He replaced his hat and mounted. "We'll take his horse with us," he added, reaching for the reins. "He left his saddlebags and rifle in camp. We can return all his stuff to his next of kin."

"That horse has a couple of minor wounds," Charvein said. "He'll need some looking after."

Belcher nodded. "I don't reckon you'll be able to ride with us." It was a statement.

"No. Got things to do."

"Too bad." Belcher sounded relieved.

Charvein touched the brim of his hat and pulled the mule around toward Lodestar. As he rode off, he felt their eyes boring into him—the tingling sensation between his shoulder blades that presaged a bullet.

But nothing happened, and he continued riding for ten minutes before venturing a look back. They were already small in the distance, moving away from him on the trail of the escapees.

It had been a foolish notion, thinking he could ever find or catch up to Denson Boyd. His pursuit of Boyd would have to wait. Right now, he'd take Lucy home, regroup, and decide his next move.

*   *   *

Buck Rankin awoke gradually, feeling like he had the worst hangover of his life. His nose was clogged, his mouth dry and tasting of dirt. He rolled over and sat up on the dust-covered floor, muscles aching. The chronic pain in his hamstring was as familiar as an old adversary.

For a minute he couldn't recall where he was or what had happened. He wiped his eyes carefully. One of them was stuck shut. When he got his eyes working, he took in his surroundings and saw he was in some sort of vacant room. The sun's rays slanted through a big shard of broken glass in one of the windows. The sun was high, just past noon.

He was suddenly seized with a paroxysm of sneezing. When he stopped, he untied his bandanna, shook it out, and blew brown dirt out of his nostrils. His head ached, his throat was parched, and his big frame felt heavy, loggy, lifeless. Thinking was an effort. Sitting on the floor, he inhaled deeply. His breath was wheezy. *Damned near drowned in dust*, he thought.

Flashes of the recent past crossed his mind. He recalled leaving the posse behind and striking out in the storm for Lodestar. That must be where he was now, but he had no clear memory of getting here. He concentrated. It was disconcerting not being able to remember everything in detail. Even in his heavier days of jousting with John Barleycorn, he'd always been able to recall everything the next day.

He remembered being terrified of something. He tried to conjure up a mental image of it. A figure . . . someone following and calling his name. Had that really happened, or was it just the wind and fatigue and his imagination? He squeezed his eyes shut. A man's frame. A familiar voice. Schooner Douglas! From his own posse. He'd panicked at the apparition and fired. Why? Fear? Anger that the big

man had followed him? Who knew? His own horse had
bolted at the gunfire. Details began to fall into place. He re-
lived the last part of that ordeal, when he had staggered up
the long slope into the teeth of the gusting wind, pushed
open a door, and fallen inside this building. He must have
passed out from exhaustion or lack of breathable air. Had
he killed Schooner Douglas? He pulled his Colt and checked
it. Three expended shells in the cylinder. Three was enough.
Even drunk, he was a good shot. If Douglas had actually
been there, he would have taken some lead.

Rankin punched out the empties, then fingered cartridges from his belt loops to reload.

"What now, Buck, old boy?" he husked aloud to himself.
He'd abandoned that no-good posse so he could operate on
his own, acting on a hunch that the two escapees were in
Lodestar. He was determined to capture or kill these two
kidnappers and rake in the entire reward.

But, first things first. He had to find water. He'd lost his
mount with the canteen on the saddle. A low flame of thirst
burned his throat. He fantasized about plunging headfirst
into the cool waters of the Carson River, cleansing his hair,
eyes, nose, and throat, if not his lungs.

He got to his feet, feeling like a wounded bear. His leg
pained him, but he hardly noticed, so much a part of his life
had it become. Walking stiffly to the front door of the vacant building, he looked out into the deserted street. At least
the dust and wind had subsided, and the sun was shining.
No one in sight. No sound. A light breeze fanned his face
as he stepped into the street. It was so quiet that to maintain
the hush he instinctively refrained from clumping along the
boardwalk. In case the men he sought were hiding somewhere in this ghost town, he didn't want to advertise his
presence. But the place felt dead. He sensed he was the only
living soul here. He ducked in and out of each building he

passed. Finally spotting a forlorn-looking saloon with one batwing door missing, he went inside.

Someone had been here recently. Lots of scuff marks and boot prints on the dirty floor. He was sure his quarry had been here. Going into the back room, he poked around through the boxes and barrels, disturbing a mouse. He found a half case of sarsaparilla and breathed a sigh while he carefully worked off the cap and tasted it. He grinned. Never had sarsaparilla tasted so good. He hauled the case out front and set it on the bar, where he emptied two bottles and started on a third before he began to feel more human. Perhaps he could find some tinned food that was still edible, although he didn't have much hope of that. Continuing his explorations, he found evidence of recent human presence in several other buildings. Piles of fairly fresh horse manure littered the streets. Several horses, at least, he thought. Deposited within the past two days. Lodestar was anything but a ghost town. After poking into most of the buildings up and down Center Street and three more on side streets, Rankin was thoroughly sick of dirt, litter, pack rat droppings, broken glass, rusting cans, and all the usual trash left to be covered by the patient dust of time.

Tired, he sat on the edge of the boardwalk on the shady side of the street. He thought of the posse and wondered if they'd started back to Virginia City. It would be more like them to be dithering and arguing about what to do and which way to go, trying to figure out if they'd been abandoned. *Amateurs*, he thought. But he had other things to occupy his mind. He'd rest a bit during the hottest part of the day, then see if he could locate his horse. Buck Rankin was tougher than dust storms, ghost towns, posses, and especially fugitives who had a big price on their heads.

Going inside a barbershop, he lay down on the floor. He was very tired. The ordeal of the night before had taken

more out of him than he liked to admit. Growing older was
not something he would do gracefully.

He dozed in the heat.

Charvein was hot, tired, and thirsty. But as Sandoval's mule
plodded into Lodestar, Charvein found himself thinking
more and more about Lucy. Pretty and young, she was a
bright spot—something nice to ponder instead of mulling
over the recent brutal episodes. During the two or three days
it would take them to ride back to Carson City, he'd get
to know her better. The trip should be uneventful, though
he couldn't bet on that. At least Sandoval, who'd observed
the weather here for four years, had assured him the night
wind would not blow again for several days. The cessation
of wind-borne dust would be a blessing.

He caught a movement, and his heart rate quickened.
But it was only a tumbleweed bouncing along to fetch up
against the front of the barbershop fifty yards ahead of him.
To the end of the street and then on to Sandoval's cavern.
He wondered what Sandoval and Lucy would say when
they saw him returning so soon.

He rode past the barbershop.

"Hands up, mister!" came a command from behind him,
accompanied by the sharp double click of a pistol being
cocked.

His heart sank.

SEVENTEEN

Not again. Twice in the same day. Could he be lucky a second time?

Slight pressure on the reins brought the tired mule to a standstill. He raised his hands to shoulder height and waited, not turning around. *I'll force him to shoot me in the back, if that's what he has in mind.*

He heard scuffing steps approach. A man holding a pistol circled around in front of him, staying several yards away.

"Sorry to do this, mister, but I have need of your mule and your water." He cleared his throat and spat while motioning with the weapon. "Get down."

Charvein dismounted and stepped to one side. There was something familiar about this man, he thought, trying to see the face shaded by the hat brim. With a jolt, he recognized Buck Rankin—older, rougher-looking, but it was the same hard man he'd known as a deputy U.S. marshal.

"Buck? Is that you?"

The man's head snapped up and he stared intently. No sign of recognition in the bloodshot eyes.

"Marc Charvein. Railroad detective a good while ago. You took a couple prisoners off my hands after they'd robbed the U.S. Mail coach back in '75."

"Is that so?"

It was obvious Rankin still didn't recall. This man had apparently been through a lot since their last meeting. "A bunch of summers have rolled over us since then. What've you been up to, Buck?"

Rankin looked confused.

Charvein had to be careful. The man's mental state might be delicate if he'd recently abandoned his posse and killed Schooner Douglas. Obviously, this wasn't the Buck Rankin he remembered.

Holding Charvein with his eyes and his Colt, Rankin moved toward the mule. "Back up."

Charvein obeyed, still trying to sound relaxed and casual. "That ain't my mule, Buck, but you can borrow him if you really need to."

Rankin led the mule a short distance away and mounted.

"You sure we've met before?"

"Hell, I'd know you anywhere, Buck." A lie. "You likely met a lot of people in your line o' work, but surely you remember me—Marc Charvein. We were both in and out of Virginia City and Gold Hill around the time the miners hit the Big Bonanza. Those were boom times, weren't they?" he kept up his familiar patter.

Rankin lowered his Colt but still held it, resting his hand on the saddle horn.

Charvein tried another tack. "Buck, if you're on the trail of those two escapees from Carson who kidnapped the girl, I can tell you where they went."

Rankin became instantly intent. "How do you know about them?"

"I was after Denson Boyd," he replied, deciding to tell

at least part of the truth. "Followed him here. Then his two ex-partners showed up with their woman hostage. We had a run-in." He took a few easy steps toward Rankin. Maybe he could catch the ex-marshal off guard and jump him. Buck's reactions seemed sluggish. "Were you riding a sorrel with a California saddle?"

"Yeah. You seen him?"

"Sure did. He was wandering loose."

"I gotta get him back."

"Too late. Those two men you're after got away with him and are headed across the playa toward Virginia City right now."

"Damn your hide! You better be tellin' me the truth." He raised his Colt again.

Charvein spread his palms to show he had nothing to hide. "If you don't believe me, I can show you their tracks on the edge of town." If he could get them all chasing the same convicts, he and Lucy could make their getaway, leaving Sandoval in his hideaway—once again the sole occupant of Lodestar.

"How long they been gone?" Rankin was more alert, attentive.

"Since just after sunup."

"Why didn't you go after them?"

Charvein shrugged. "They weren't my worry. I was deputized to find Boyd. But he escaped in another direction last night."

Rankin's eyes narrowed, and he seemed to focus. "Drop your gunbelt."

"What for? Buck, you and I are on the same side of the law."

"I'm borrowing your mule, whether you like it or not. If I get my horse, I'll turn this animal loose to find its way back to you—provided you got him trained right." He raised his Colt again. "Show me those tracks, and I'll decide if they were made by the two I'm looking for."

Charvein had a sense of events repeating themselves as he unbuckled his gunbelt and let it fall at his feet. "Follow me." He turned and began walking toward the upper end of the street.

He'd gone only ten yards when a rifle shot cracked.

Eeee-Haww!!!

Charvein whirled in time to see the mule jump and buck. Rankin's Colt went flying as he grabbed for the saddle horn with both hands.

Another shot from somewhere took Rankin's hat off. The mule leapt up and down in a jolting, stiff-legged panic, flinging the ex-marshal out of the saddle. Rankin rolled out of the way of the flying hooves and grabbed his pistol out of the dust. He scrambled toward the gaping doorway of the nearest building. Another shot tore splinters from the hitching rail a foot behind the fleeing man.

Charvein had no time to look for the origin of the shots, but he sensed they weren't meant for him as he dodged desperately around the mule, trying to retrieve his gunbelt on the ground.

The mule finally galloped off toward the lower end of Center Street, and Charvein grabbed his gunbelt just as a slug kicked up dust close to his hand. The shot came from Rankin's direction; Charvein sprinted the opposite way, throwing himself behind the corner of the stone church.

Panting, he crouched, pulled his weapon, and scanned the buildings. Another rifle shot blasted the stillness, and he saw the puff of smoke come from behind a ruined watering trough fifty yards away. Who the hell was that?

Rankin had apparently spotted the smoke as well, and he returned fire. But he was out of effective pistol range.

A figure sprang up from behind the trough and dashed

between two buildings. In the two seconds of exposure, Charvein recognized the faded brown and red poncho. Sandoval!

Charvein fired two quick shots toward Rankin's hiding place, then sprinted through the open front door of the church. A minute later, Sandoval entered the nave from a side door near the ruined baptistry.

"You don't have to help me," Charvein said. "I think I can probably handle Buck Rankin. He's out of his head."

"Rankin!" The name slithered from Sandoval's lips like the foulest curse. His black, hooded eyes were reptilian, set in a face of stone.

"You know him, too? He acts like he doesn't remember me from our lawman days."

"Does a sinner not know Satan?"

Charvein wondered what stirred such venom as the two of them slid up to either side of the open doorway and looked across the street. There was no sign of Rankin.

Charvein noted the rifle in Sandoval's hands. "You could have hit him dead center with that," he said, recalling the shot in the dirt that spooked the mule, and the second bullet that had taken off Buck's hat.

"Could have," he replied, clenching his jaw.

For a moment, Charvein didn't speak. "Buck was acting strange, but I don't think he'd have shot me. He ordered me to point out the tracks of the two escapees he was hunting. I put his posse on the same trail a couple miles out on the playa earlier today." He looked at Sandoval's impassive face, trying to assess his motivation. "You didn't want to shoot him from ambush just to get your mule back— I understand that. But now we have to deal with him, somehow."

*   *   *

Sandoval remained silent, staring across the street at the weathered building that sheltered Buck Rankin.

"That was Rankin's horse we found and sold this morning," Charvein added. "I was just trying to get Buck out of town and chasing the same tracks. Then we'd be rid of them all."

Something else was eating at Sandoval. "Buck Rankin is the reason I'm here in Lodestar." He paused, and Charvein concealed his surprise as he waited for him to continue.

"Rankin forced himself on my wife . . . threatened her with a knife . . . I walked in on him having his way with her . . ." He struggled to force out this information in short, breathless bursts. "Shot at him in bed. Wounded him in the leg. But I was half-drunk and blind with hate, and my bullets went wild and hit her, too . . ." Sandoval was breathing hard now, slim hands convulsing on the rifle stock. "That damned Rankin howled like the very devil himself. Blood everywhere . . . I scooped up my wife and ran. Threw her across my saddle and rode like the wind . . . She was dead even then, but I didn't know it." He choked back a sob. "I was a wanted man . . . Shook off a posse in the mountains . . . Caught a wild burro, managed to reach Lodestar. Buried my wife near here in a secret place. Almost starved at first. Survived on rabbits and gopher rats." He drew a deep breath and looked at Charvein. "I'll be hanged for murder if I go back."

Charvein absorbed this shock, then said, "Surely any jury would consider what you did justifiable."

"No. A dark-skinned man can't shoot a deputy U.S. marshal and walk free, no matter the circumstances."

"Any witnesses?"

Sandoval shook his head. "His word against mine. And he has friends who will back up his story."

Charvein knew he was right. "Where did this happen?"

"Little place called Chilton, Nevada, south of Carson. A

mining town where Buck Rankin came to escort a prisoner back to Virginia City for trial. He thought my Linda was fair game because she was a cook in a cantina."

He let this sink in. "How do you keep from being recognized and arrested when you make trips to Virginia City for supplies?"

"Thousands of people come and go there all the time. This happened four years ago. I have a friend in Virginia City who lets me stay at his casa while he takes my money and buys my supplies. I come and go by night. As time passes, my crime has been forgotten, by everyone except me—and Rankin."

Charvein wanted to probe for more details. But tears formed in Sandoval's eyes, and his Adam's apple worked as he tried to swallow his emotion. Not the time for more questions.

"Maybe we can just run him off," Charvein suggested, sounding unconvincing even to himself.

"My mule has run back toward the cavern," Sandoval said. "If we can smoke Rankin out, and disarm him, we'll give him a canteen and send him across the playa on foot."

Charvein glanced at his friend. "Might as well shoot him. It'd be more merciful than sending him out there to die. He's been through quite an ordeal already; he'd never make it across."

"Why should I care about that? My heart is stone. We'll give him a chance. If God wants to save him, He can."

"But you couldn't bring yourself to shoot him?"

"Then or now?"

"Either."

"I meant to do it then, but I was in a blind rage and I missed killing him."

"Did you intend to kill your wife?"

He shook his head slowly, his eyes staring into space

outside. "No," he almost whispered. "It has haunted me every day since then. I was drinking and my aim was bad. Much later I was told by a friend who was in the cantina that night that when she refused money Rankin offered— dollars we desperately needed—he forced her into the back room with a knife and took her against her will."

"Can this friend be your witness in court?"

"He has since died."

Charvein had only an inkling of the pain such a situation would bring.

"Not a day goes by that I do not grieve for her and for my terrible sin. Her unmarked grave is near my cave." The criminal aspect of the killing apparently didn't concern him. "I went to confession later in Virginia City, and the priest told me I was not to blame because it was an accident. Still, I cannot undo what I did. It eats at me every day. One day my guilt will kill me."

"If God holds you blameless, then you are blameless. Why can't you accept that?"

Sandoval drew a long breath. "I was not blameless. I was drunk and I had murder in my heart when I shot at Rankin. My punishment is that I killed my beloved wife instead. Maybe someday . . . I have spent my purgatory here. It will continue until my bones rest in this desert."

The crucial part of Sandoval's past had finally been revealed. At least some of the mystery of this recluse was solved.

"She is buried nearby where I can go and visit her grave and ask her forgiveness," Sandoval was saying.

"I'm sure she knows how you feel," Charvein said, trying to console him. Mental anguish had to be even worse than many types of physical pain. He glanced toward the sanctuary of the old church and saw where the altar had been covered with a white cloth. Two candles thrust into the necks of wine bottles stood on either end of the altar. A small crucifix hung on the wall behind. Evidently, Sandoval had fashioned his own place of worship in this crumbling building.

He turned his attention back to business. But he was a fraction too late to prevent Sandoval from stepping out the open doorway into the bright sunlight of the street. "Sandoval! Get back here!" Did he have a death wish?

Sandoval threw his poncho back over his right shoulder, freeing his gun hand that still gripped the lever-action rifle at his side. "Buck Rankin!" he shouted. "You sniveling, wife-stealing bastard, show your cowardly hide."

A few seconds of silence ensued, then there was movement in the shadow of the boardwalk, and the ex-marshal stepped out into the bright light, Colt thrust forward in a big fist.

"How's your leg?" Sandoval taunted. "You think of me every time you try to stand up from a chair? That leg give out when you dismount from a horse? Does the pain keep you up at night—give you an excuse for another drink?" An oily laugh sent chills up Charvein's back. "You ever see my wife's blood in your dreams? Well, take a good look at me!" He thumped his chest with his free hand. "At me—the man who shot you."

"Should have known a half-breed snake would someday come crawling out from under a rock," Buck snarled. He seemed to have recovered his addled senses. "So this is where you went to ground. It'll give me and my leg great satisfaction to finally leave your rotten carcass for the buzzards."

Charvein was fascinated by the deadly drama that was playing out before him. As the lone, unwilling audience member, he seemed paralyzed to interfere. Was this old animosity destined to end here and now?

The hammer of Sandoval's downward-pointing rifle was cocked, and his forefinger was inside the trigger guard. But he could never bring it up and fire before Rankin could cock and squeeze off a shot from the pistol he held at waist level. The two men stood thirty feet apart. The silence of eternity stretched between them.

EIGHTEEN

"Sandoval!"

All three heads snapped toward the woman's scream.

"Lucy, stay back!" Charvein yelled. But the bare legs continued flashing toward them in the sunlight, her black hair flying, torn blue dress flapping.

The taut thread of deadly tension snapped. Rankin stepped back, mouth agape at this apparition, gun hand falling to his side.

Charvein glimpsed all this in a second and leapt out the door, grabbing Sandoval by the arm and jerking him back inside.

Within seconds, Lucy dashed in to join them, gasping, breasts heaving, eyes wide.

A pistol roared, and a slug tore splinters from the big door frame as Rankin recovered too late from his shock.

"I heard shots," she panted. "Had to find out if Sandoval was all right. And now you're here, too." She reached out for Charvein.

He gave her hand a quick squeeze. "That couldn't have

been better timed if you'd been the ghost of Schooner Douglas," he said, pulling her farther behind the protective front wall.

"Who?" she gasped.

"Never mind. I'll explain later."

Sandoval's hands trembled. He nervously licked his lips. "I would have shot him . . . I would have killed him," he muttered. "I haven't changed at all."

"More likely he'd have killed you," Charvein said, eyeing his friend. What was Sandoval's mental state? Did he have a good enough grip on his nerves to see this thing through? Charvein knew it was up to him to protect the other two. He had to do something about getting rid of Rankin. But how? If Sandoval hadn't interfered when he did, Rankin would be gone on the mule by now. True, Sandoval would have lost his animal, but they still had the burro and food and water. The three of them could have managed, somehow.

"You're all right?" Lucy's question was not routine; the concern in her voice was genuine.

"Except for a bump on the head and lack of sleep, I'm fine," Charvein assured her.

She let out a long sigh and her breathing began to steady. "I was so worried." She stepped forward and gave him a convulsive hug.

Charvein was embarrassed, but pleased, by her sudden show of affection.

"I'm in good shape," he said, taking her by the shoulders and gently pushing her away from him. "But now we have to deal with our next problem—how to capture or run off that ex-marshal across the street." He went on to give her a brief summary of what had transpired. In the meantime, Sandoval was keeping watch on Rankin's hiding place.

"Any sign of him?" Charvein asked, stepping to Sandoval's side.

"I heard him moving around, but he hasn't shown himself."

"Well, we've got to do something. We can't stay here from now on."

"Neither can he."

"Look, why don't you slip out through the sanctuary and go find your mule. Lucy and I can keep an eye on Rankin." It would relieve Charvein to have his agitated friend out of the way for now. Maybe he would calm down while he was rounding up the animal.

"That mule won't go far. Probably grazing near the cavern right now," Sandoval said.

"Best round him up, yank that saddle off, and give him some grain. He carried me a long way today."

"Verdad."

"When you get back, we'll try to outflank Rankin. Bring a gun back for Lucy."

Sandoval nodded.

"Rankin's not in the best of shape, physically or mentally. The three of us should be able to capture him." Charvein tried to sound confident, but Sandoval was obviously having none of it.

"He's one mean . . . !" Sandoval spat out something in Spanish Charvein didn't understand, but he was just as glad he didn't. Sandoval eased the Henry's hammer down and tossed the rifle into the crook of his arm. His hands no longer trembled. He seemed to have regained control of himself.

"I know he's no pushover, but I think we can figure out a way to get hold of him without any of us getting hurt."

Sandoval headed toward the side door off the sanctuary.

"By the way, is there a way to reach the belfry?"

Sandoval stopped and turned, hooded eyes probing. "Why?"

"If I can get a higher angle, we can catch him in a cross fire. He won't be looking for anything coming at him from up there." He shrugged. "Possibly wing him. The Buck Rankin I knew won't give up without a fight."

Sandoval glanced up toward the bell tower, then back at Charvein. "Why is he even fighting us?"

"Because you're an old enemy who gave him that leg wound." Charvein thought it better not to mention the wife.

"The stairway was falling apart and wasn't safe. I tore it down and used it for firewood last January."

"Well, it was just an idea."

"But I built a wooden ladder to replace the steps," Sandoval continued. "It's over in that far corner. I nailed it in place, but you have to be careful. Not sure it's real sturdy. Haven't used it for months."

"Okay."

"I'll be back after I take care of the mule—sooner if I hear gunfire." He ghosted past the makeshift altar, toward a rear door leading to the alley.

NINETEEN

Buck Rankin was still feeling muzzy in the head. His thinking seemed dull. All he wanted to do was lie down and close his eyes. But no time for that now. His confrontation with Sandoval had been interrupted by some crazy woman who came screaming out of nowhere. Lodestar must be crawling with ghosts—or with more live people than he ever expected. Where in hell had she come from, and who was she? She sounded terrified, shouting Sandoval's name, as if he were about to be cut down by a bullet. And he likely would have been, Rankin thought, fingering the warm steel of the Colt in his hand.

Sandoval's new wife. That was it. The greaser had found himself another woman, and they'd been hiding out in this ghost town. *Then why am I still fighting Sandoval over his first wife, Linda—a woman long dead?* As soon as the thought crossed his mind, he knew that wasn't it. He didn't know if Sandoval had intended to kill her, but one of the bullets from the Mex had sure as hell ruined Buck Rankin's career as a deputy marshal.

Good thing Sandoval had taken off without waiting to defend himself in court. It could've gotten messy for Rankin if the story about the seduction had come out. No good for a lawman's reputation. He and Sandoval were the only ones who knew exactly what had happened in the back room of that cantina. And if he could kill those three across the street, no one else ever would. He had a vague recollection of the man who called himself Charvein. He'd run into him a time or two years before.

Sitting on the floor to ease the strain on his leg that was paining him more than usual, he leaned back against the wall. Normally in full control of himself, he now felt an unsettling mix of emotions. It had started in the night with the appearance of Schooner Douglas, or something that looked and sounded like Schooner. Perhaps it was his own imagination or conscience he'd been shooting at. It was this dust—this damned dust and wind—that caused a man to doubt his senses, to lose his grip on reality. The heaviness in his chest reminded Rankin he was carrying a load of powdery soil from that dry playa. He wasn't yet dead, but he felt as if he'd been buried from the inside out.

If he killed Sandoval, the man who'd given him this never-healing wound and ended his career, he *knew* he'd feel much better. The leg would not be one whit less painful, but the satisfaction of laying low that damned greaser would make up for it.

A horse snorted. Rankin jerked out of his reverie. He'd heard nothing from across the street for a time; were they trying to sneak up behind him? Surely they'd be coming afoot—not on horseback. He crawled to the open door and peered out. A horseman was halted eighty yards away, the man's face hidden in shadow under a wide hat brim. Although the town was silent, the rider must have sensed something, as he sat quietly surveying the empty street, a rifle resting across his pommel. He was riding a mule and trailing another with a pack saddle. Neither of the animals was the same one Charvein had. The man was tall—not a member of his posse.

Another damned stranger. The man looked wary, and he was armed. Buck instantly abandoned thoughts of killing Sandoval. With surprise on his side, he felt he could waylay this man and take both his mules. Becoming mobile again took precedence over everything else. With transportation, he could find food and water and then get back on the track of those two escapees who represented his reward. Revenge would have to wait.

Gripping his Colt, he eased back until he could barely see the rider through the wavy glass of a nearby window. After a long minute, the rider urged his mount forward at a walk, scanning the buildings on either side as he came. How to take him? Buck knew he couldn't expose himself, for fear of being shot from across the street. He'd wait until the rider passed, then use him as a shield against the church where Sandoval, Charvein, and the woman were hiding. It was risky, but worth the chance; he had to have at least one of those mules, along with any water the man might be carrying.

On came the mule and rider, and Buck used the wall to push himself erect, gingerly putting weight on his painful leg.

As the stranger passed him, Buck stepped into the street. "Stop right there and drop that rifle!" he commanded in a throaty voice.

The rider stiffened and, without turning, began to lower his rifle.

A shot blasted the stillness and a bullet clipped Buck's boot sole. "Ahh!" He jumped back. Smoke drifted from the bell tower of the church. They were above him.

The rider's mule reared as a second shot zinged past the animal's ear. The rider dove off, still gripping his rifle, turned a somersault in the dirt, and both he and Buck dashed for the shelter of an open door.

Two more bullets slammed into the wall as they tumbled inside. The mules plunged away up the street.

Buck managed to get the drop on the startled stranger. "Just set that long gun down, easy-like," he said, earing back the hammer on his own gun.

The man laid the rifle down, and Buck reached forward with his left hand and removed the Colt from the man's holster. He shoved the gun under his own belt. "Stay away from that door and window. Some folks across the street are gunning for me."

"So it was you they were shooting at," the man said. "I thought they were mighty poor shots, or were just trying to scare me."

Buck nodded, eyeing this rugged-looking man. "Who're you?"

The man hesitated slightly, glancing at Buck's leveled handgun. "Denson Boyd," he replied.

The name struck no chords with Buck. "How'd you come to be in this deserted place?"

"Look, I have no quarrel with you," Boyd said. "You can put the gun down. If it's money you want, I have a few dollars in my pocket. You're welcome to whatever I got."

"I don't want your money. I wanted one of your animals so I could get the hell outta here," Buck replied.

"Looks like we're both out of luck on that score," Boyd replied, glancing outside.

"You didn't answer my question. What're you doing in Lodestar?"

"Give me your story first. You got me disarmed. We can talk. Who are you?"

Buck instinctively liked the confidence of this man. "My name is Buck Rankin. I was leading a posse after two escapees from the Carson City prison—men name of Marty Stepenaw and Glen Savage, known as the Weasel."

"What?" Boyd's eyes flew open. "I'll be damned. You know why they busted out of prison? They were coming after me. I was pardoned by the governor, but they thought I knew where the money was we took from a train a few years back. Even if I knew where it was, I wasn't about to touch none o' that stolen gold. No siree!"

Buck had dealt with enough lying criminals to know this last statement was only for the record and contained no truth.

Boyd squinted at him. "So you're Buck Rankin, the famous deputy marshal?"

"I'm Rankin, all right. But hardly famous. You heard of me?"

"Who hasn't?"

Buck began to feel better about himself than he had for months. Maybe his career as a lawman hadn't been completely in vain.

"You'll never believe what happened to me today."

Buck arched his eyebrows.

"Before I tell you, let's have a drink. I want to be able to say I had a drink with Buck Rankin." He very slowly reached into his side jacket pocket and drew out a metal flask. "Can't never tell when you might fall off your horse, so it's not a good idea to carry glass bottles around in your pocket." He unscrewed the cap and held out the big flask.

Buck hesitated, not sure if he could trust this ex-convict. Why was the man being so friendly?

"It's okay. If you're a drinking man, this is pretty good stuff."

Buck finally reached for the flask, tipped it up, and took

a small swallow. Boyd had told the truth. Eyes and gun muzzle still locked on Boyd, Buck took a longer pull. The liquor went down smooth, then exploded silently in his gut, spreading warmth. He handed the flask back.

"Might as well put the gun down. Looks like we're both in the same fix."

"You could walk out of here and they wouldn't shoot you," Buck said.

"Not so sure about that. Why they after you?"

"Me and that fella, Sandoval, over there, got some old personal business to settle."

"Where's your posse?" Boyd took a swig from his flask.

"If you want the truth, I ditched 'em 'cause they were city softies got forced on me. I figured to make the arrest and collect all the reward money myself. But then that dust storm caught me and I lost my horse. Wound up here and found an old enemy instead of the two I was hunting." He took the flask from Boyd and had another swallow. The liquor was working its magic already. Even his leg was less painful. Now if he just had some food . . . "So, why are you here?" He coughed and spat dirt on the bare floor. Holstering his Colt, he backed away several feet, remaining wary in case this Boyd was trying to lull him into letting down his guard to jump him.

But Boyd sat down, cross-legged on the floor, even neglecting to retrieve his flask. "I don't think you're going to get the reward for capturing those two convicts," he said.

"Why's that?"

"Because your posse has them in shackles, and they're heading for Carson City right now."

"What?" The enormity of this statement cut through the haze that was beginning to form over Buck's caution. "How d'you know that?" Anger flared within him. This Boyd seemed entirely too sure of himself.

"Earlier today I ran into them several miles out that way." He jerked his head toward the west. "I was here in Lodestar, and last night I slipped out and took the horses of my two ex-partners and their woman hostage so they couldn't trail me. Strung their mounts together behind my pack mule and started for Virginia City. After a couple miles, I realized I didn't have enough water to see me and the animals all the way to Virginia City." He leaned his back against the wall and straightened his legs in front of him. "Heard some gunfire off in the distance. Yanked my field glasses and spotted Stepenaw and Savage with one horse, trying to fend off three riders coming up on them. It was no contest. Knew it had to be a posse who captured them—yours? I rode up and gave the three horses to the posse so they'd have enough animals to carry their two prisoners back to Carson. Stepenaw and Savage accused me of having some stolen gold, but I denied any knowledge of it, and then showed my letter of pardon from the governor."

Buck silently struggled to absorb this. His reward gone— just like that—fallen into the hands of his stupid posse. What dumb luck!

"Then I headed back here with my mules to stock up on water before making another try for Virginia City," Boyd added.

Buck didn't know what to think. Here was a completely new turn of events. Maybe he could partner up with this man until they could both return to civilization. No sooner had the thought crossed his mind than Boyd said, "You lost the reward you were after." It was not an accusation—only a statement of fact.

"Yeah."

Boyd took a deep breath. "I know you're a lawman and all . . ."

"Retired lawman," Buck interrupted him.

"But, if you happen to be interested, I might have an idea that could benefit both of us."

"What's that?"

"I served four years in the state pen, so I figure I paid my debt to society. Four years of my life at hard labor ought to be worth something."

"What're you getting at?" Buck paused to glance across the street toward the church bell tower, but the shooter was not to be seen.

"I had no intention of touching any of that stolen gold from the robbery, but the way I look at it, I'm due some of it as pay for the time I served."

Buck suddenly became all ears. "You know where it is?"

"Might, and I might not. But I first need your word you won't double-cross me."

"My word might not be worth a chaw o' tobbaco."

"Nevertheless, I have to trust you. You might say both of us are in a bind right now."

Buck considered this. "You offering to split with me?"

"Might do, if I have your word."

Partnering up with a criminal to share in stolen gold was hardly the way Buck Rankin had expected to end his career. But living on stolen money was better than surviving on handouts. He cringed at the vision of himself cadging drinks and begging on the street, until someone found his stiff carcass in an alleyway some icy morning. He would do whatever it took to avoid such a fate. After all, a man had to play the cards he was dealt, and this Boyd was dealing, when all other plans and schemes had failed. "Okay, you got my solemn word I won't try to arrest you. I accept your offer to share. But tell me this . . . why you offering this to me? I have no reason to keep you, no authority to hold you prisoner, now that you been pardoned. Once you leave here you can take off and get the gold without sharing with anyone."

"I didn't want to give you one of my animals and be forced to accompany you back to Virginia City to get it back."

"That's not the reason."

Boyd sighed. "You're right. The fact is, I don't know where the gold is."

"So this is some pie-in-the-sky tale—one of those lost mine fables, where the pot of gold at the end of the rainbow is just beyond your reach." He snorted, disgusted he'd fallen for something that was obviously too good to be true, although he did remember newspaper accounts at the time of the trial mentioning the unrecovered ingots.

If Boyd took any offense at this outburst, he gave no indication of it. "Here's how it came about," he said. "When I came back here to Nightwind Canyon, where we'd stashed the gold a few years ago, it was gone—the cave was clean as a whistle, like there'd never been any gold in it at all. Then my two former partners showed up and accused me of hiding it from them. We got into it and . . . well, you don't care about all that." He gave a dismissive wave of his hand. "The rock bottom truth of the matter is, I don't have any idea where that gold got to. But now those two ex-partners of mine are on their way back to jail and out of the way." He stood up and stretched. "I came back to Lodestar because I'm convinced the ingots are still here. Your posse found Stepenaw and Weasel carrying part of a gold ingot they claimed to have found near a cave where they'd held me prisoner. They accused me of dropping it there when I escaped with the rest of the stash."

He paused, and Rankin tried to absorb all this quickly and decide if the man was telling the truth.

"And half of anything we find is yours if you'll help me

shake this old ghost town upside down until that gold falls out. If we don't find it, then neither one of us is any worse off than we are now."

Buck prided himself on being able to read men. He'd been fooled a time or two over the years by professional confidence men. Even though Denson Boyd seemed guileless, that didn't mean he was. Buck knew the facts of the robbery to be true, but Boyd might be lying about everything else. Buck decided he had little to lose; he might as well take a chance. He tipped up the flask for another long swig as he made up his mind. Then he limped across to the man on the floor and thrust out his hand. "Done!" He handed Boyd's Colt back to him. "Before we can start, we gotta figure out a way to get rid of those three across the street."

TWENTY

The murmur of voices caused Charvein to glance down from his perch behind the balustrade that surrounded the bell tower. Lucy and Sandoval were conversing near the foot of the ladder. Charvein hadn't heard him return. Sandoval, in his moccasins, moved with a feline fluidity that was virtually silent.

Charvein removed his hat and inched his eyes just above the edge of the bulwark. There was no sign of the two men across the street. He hoped the pair had escaped unseen out the back door of the empty building where they hid. He didn't care about killing either one of them; he just wanted them gone. He'd fired to barely miss and put them on the defensive. Why the hell had Denson Boyd come back to Lodestar? And where were the three horses he'd stolen when he'd disappeared that night into the blowing dust?

Charvein crawfished to the trapdoor and slid his legs through the hole onto the top step of the homemade ladder. It felt good to stretch as he climbed down.

"What do you have for us?" he asked as Sandoval handed him a cloth sack.

"Tortillas and beans," he said, then gestured toward two bulbous, wicker-encased bottles on the floor. "Water and wine."

Charvein's stomach growled at the aroma of the food, and he grinned.

"All the comforts of home. We can outlast a siege." Even as he said it, he was hoping for a quick end to this standoff.

"*Sí.*" Sandoval nodded solemnly. "We have provisions, and they do not."

Lucy hefted the big six-gun Sandoval had brought for her. "Do you have extra cartridges for this?" she asked as she flipped open the loading gate, half-cocked the hammer, and turned the cylinder to be sure it was loaded. Charvein was relieved at her familiar ease with firearms; her father had taught her well.

"*Sí.*" He produced a box of .45 cartridges from one of the inside pockets of his poncho. "I do not often need these when I am here alone," he said. "But Lodestar has had much company lately."

"We better keep watch on that building across the way," Charvein said to Sandoval. "Take a peek around the door, but crawl up and keep your head on the floor. That way, if either of them is sighted in on the doorway, waiting to blow somebody's head off as soon as it appears, he won't see you soon enough."

"*Sí.*" Sandoval turned, but Lucy grabbed his arm. "Let me do it."

Sandoval looked appealingly to Charvein, who nodded. "It's okay." He was secretly proud that she was finally becoming part of their team and wanted to share in the danger and responsibility. Maybe a real experience with fighting and peril would knock some of that medieval romantic nonsense out of her head.

Lucy dropped to her hands and knees and, holding the pistol, crawled to the tall open doorway, where she lay flat and eased her head around the edge. Five seconds later she pulled back and stood up. "No sign of them. The mules are gone, too—maybe gone around the bend at the end of the street."

Charvein thought for a moment. "It's about two o'clock," he estimated. "What do you say we give them till dark to make a move. I'm guessing they'll try to get us, or try to escape, by then. They won't want to just sit over there all night in the dark, without food or water, wondering if we're trying to sneak up on them."

"And if darkness comes and they have done nothing— what then?" Sandoval asked.

Charvein bit his lip thoughtfully, not having a ready answer. "Let's wait and see," he said. "I'll go back up to the bell tower and keep watch for a couple hours. Wrap a tortilla around some beans and give me a canteen, and I'll be fine."

"I can watch from up there, since I have a rifle," Sandoval said, hefting the Henry.

"No offense, but I'm a better shot with a pistol than you are with a rifle," Charvein replied, not mentioning his latest feat two nights before when he'd taken the head clean off a snake. "You two keep watch from down here." He'd be cautious organizing their defense, since he wasn't sure if Sandoval's rage had cooled. If the men across the street came out, Charvein didn't want Sandoval firing down on them like shooting fish in a tub, out of control with hate, possibly killing two men unnecessarily. Of course, Sandoval could do the same from down here, but it was just as likely they'd shoot him first.

"If they come out, shall we shoot?" Lucy asked.

"Yes, but only if they come out shooting. If they try to rush the church, shoot to kill," Charvein said. "Otherwise, if they're running away, let them go."

"No, señor," Sandoval said, shaking his head. "Is not a good idea. If they run away, they will hide somewhere else in town. It is like letting two rattlers loose in a dark room. We will not see them or know where they will strike."

"If we leave them alone, they'll find Boyd's mules and leave," Lucy said.

"No. Buck Rankin wants me. He would not go if we gave him the animals and *mucho* food and water." He squatted on the floor and began laying out the small pot of beans and the tortillas.

"Perhaps you're right," Charvein said, resting a foot on the bottom rung of the ladder. He was unsure of the depth of hate between Rankin and Sandoval. He marveled that hate and love could spur human effort far beyond anything logical. And greed wasn't far behind. "If I'm any judge, Boyd came back to Lodestar because he's convinced the gold is still here someplace."

"So neither of them really wants to escape from Lodestar, or from us," Lucy said, thoughtfully.

"That's what we have to assume, if we don't want to be caught off guard," Charvein said, accepting a tortilla from Sandoval. He shouldered a canteen and started up the ladder.

Ensconced behind the dried, splintery wood that enclosed the lower part of the bell tower, Charvein settled in to enjoy his meal. The old adage "Hunger makes the best sauce" popped into his mind as he devoured the simple beans and flat bread. He hadn't realized how hungry he was; he could have easily eaten three of them. Finished and still hungry, he wiped his mouth with his sleeve and gulped a few swallows of the warm, metallic-tasting canteen water. A feast fit for a king.

He leaned forward and put his eye to a gap in the warped wood. No sense exposing any part of himself to watch the building across the street. The forlorn structure appeared deserted. Charvein knew better. Only if he wanted to shoot would he have to rise above the rim of the waist-high barricade.

The church was built from slabs of native stone, but the bell tower was constructed of wood to avoid excessive weight. The cream-colored paint had long since been blistered and scoured off by the relentless sun and blowing sand. Traces of the original color survived only in protected cracks. Charvein looked up at the tarnished brass bell, its flared bottom three feet above his head. The bell was suspended from a thick oak beam supported on either end by the upright wooden frame of the tower. He idly speculated how long it would take before the weathered supports surrendered to the ravages of time and the elements. He hoped the heavy bell would stay in place for at least a few more hours. It had withstood years of winds that funneled into town through Nightwind Canyon and gusted off the vast playa. The wood had shrunk and cracked and weathered to a uniform gray, but still it stood, defiant, holding the weighty bell. Had it not been for the wind blowing the twin clappers against the bell, causing a mellow tolling, Charvein would never have been guided to Lodestar. He'd heard that bell in the night and staggered toward its sound, blinded and choking. Fate could turn on the smallest things.

He'd never seen a bell with twin clappers. These were identical, suspended six inches apart. He saw the marks of a hammer that had flattened the end of each into a rough circular shape. He guessed a bell rope had once been attached and dropped down the ladder so a sexton below could

ring the Angelus or announce Mass to Lodestar. Yet, somehow, Lodestar didn't strike him as having been a particu-
larly religious place.

In spite of the danger, Charvein couldn't keep up the intense vigil for long. The food, wine, and the silence made
his tired body sag, and his thoughts began wandering to
other things. What of his future when all this was over? He
had few prospects—to be truthful, no prospects. The idea
of continuing in some kind of law enforcement was dis-
tasteful. He'd thought he was done with that line of work
when he'd resigned from being a railroad detective. But
then he was caught up in tracking Boyd, in what he'd
thought would be a routine job. Little did he know. Maybe
he'd get his pay as a temporary deputy from the county and
also the man whose gold he was trying to find. And there
might even be a reward from Lucy's relatives—provided he
could return her, unharmed, to Carson City. He'd look for
some kind of work that would tax his brain rather than his
muscle and his guile. Leaving Virginia City seemed a good
idea, since he had no interest in mining or storekeeping.
Maybe move somewhere, like California, that had a milder
climate. Make a fresh start.

A rifle shot shattered the stillness, and a bullet whanged
off the brass bell overhead. The bell reverberated like a
tuning fork. Heart pounding, Charvein flattened himself
against the inside of the wooden bulwark. Colt in hand, he
looked through the crack and saw smoke drifting from one
of the broken windows. He waited. Maybe they were trying
to scare him out so he'd expose himself to a clear shot.

"You all right?" Sandoval called.

"Yeah." He crawled to the trapdoor at the head of the
ladder. "Keep an eye on that window. If they start shooting
again, return fire," he said softly. Then he eased back to the

base of the low barricade. He thought the wood was thick enough to stop a bullet.

Less than a minute later, two weapons opened up from across the street, the shots coming so fast they blended into a single roar that lasted several seconds. The bell clanged madly as the lead slugs ricocheted off the brass. A sliver of wood or metal stung Charvein's cheek. All he could do was crouch, arms over his head, and wait it out. The fusillade halted suddenly, but his ears continued to ring. Penetrating his partial deafness were the closer sounds of shots from below as Sandoval and Lucy returned fire.

"Marc! Marc! Are you hit?" Lucy's voice quavered.

He crawled over to the opening. "No, just a scratch on the cheek. What about you?"

"They were shooting at the tower only," Sandoval said, looking up from the bottom of the ladder.

"Trying to get me with a ricochet," Charvein agreed. "Be sure to stay behind the wall down there."

"Better come down," Sandoval said.

"In a minute." Gripping his Colt, Charvein crawled back into position. Whatever ambivalent feelings he'd had about Boyd and Rankin were long gone. They had no compunction about killing. He'd have to defend himself and his friends below by whatever means available.

Another shot exploded, and a bullet whanged off one of the clappers and hit the bell, deflecting straight down into the floor of the platform.

More shots rang out from below as Sandoval and Lucy fired back from the doorway.

Then came a lull in the firing. Charvein sat with his back to the low barricade, catching his breath. The westering sun slanted into the bell tower, picking out small details he hadn't noticed before. The suspended clappers had been recently painted a dull brown. From a distance they blended with the dark, tarnished brass of the bell. Why would anyone paint them? They were obviously handmade—possibly iron replacements that could rust. What the direct sunlight highlighted were two gouge marks where bullets had slashed across the flattened ends of the clappers. The metal beneath was not iron. It gleamed a dull yellow, but Charvein was certain it wasn't brass.

Time to get out of his exposed position. He thrust his gun hand up over the barricade and fired two quick shots in the direction of the enemy. Then he scuttled to the trapdoor and started down the ladder.

Return shots zinged off the bell, but Charvein was out of reach of the gunfire as he reached the bottom and stepped away. Lucy and Sandoval stood on either side of the open doorway, exchanging sporadic fire with the men across the street. Lucy paused and stepped back to reload.

"Charvein, if we can keep them shooting, they will run out of ammunition before we do," Sandoval said. "I have more at my cave but could not carry all I wanted to bring."

Charvein grunted his assent, his mind elsewhere as he tried to grasp pieces of a puzzle and pull them into place. But they swirled just out of his mental reach.

Lucy snapped the loading gate of her revolver shut and looked up. "Marc, you're hurt!" She approached and touched the drying blood on his cheek.

He barely heard her. "Sandoval, what are those bell clappers made of?"

Sandoval continued facing away from him, crouching beside the doorway and sneaking a look at the building across the street. "Brass . . . iron. I do not know. *No es importante*. We have men trying to kill us just now."

"Did you paint those clappers?"

"Why do you ask?" Sandoval got to his feet and turned toward him.

"They've been recently painted. The paint is not yet worn."

"Yes, I painted them. I like the sound of the bell and do what I can to keep it in good condition. I have many hours to fill when I am here alone."

"If you like the sound, why didn't you attach a rope so you could ring it from down here?"

"The wind rings it when God wants it rung."

"Perhaps He does, and the notes have a golden tone, *verdad*?" He gazed hard at Sandoval's impassive face.

"What do you mean?" The hooded eyes gave no hint of what was behind them.

"I mean those clappers are made of gold."

Lucy suppressed a gasp and looked from one to the other.

Sandoval shrugged. "I suppose they are. I had to do something with those ingots."

"You mean . . ." Lucy's eyes were wide.

"Yes," Charvein said, not taking his eyes from Sandoval. "For days, men have been running around, fighting each other, looking for that golden stash. And all the time it was hanging in the belfry of this church."

TWENTY-ONE

For a few moments the three of them stared at one another, the gunmen across the street forgotten.

Sandoval was the key to this all along. As the shock wore off, a feeling of betrayal crept over Charvein. Betrayed by a man he'd thought his friend and benefactor. But this feeling quickly passed when he realized Sandoval didn't have to save his life at all, or give him food and water, shelter him from the dust storm, hide him from his enemies. He took a deep breath. If their situations had been reversed, Charvein would've done the same. "Then you were the one who left that gold ingot where Stepenaw and Weasel would find it by the cave?"

"*Sí.* I wanted to distract them, so I could perhaps try a rescue. I didn't know Boyd had already released you."

"Thanks." Charvein was sorry for his anger. "When did you find the gold?"

"Only weeks after I first came here. About four years ago. I explored every inch of this town. The bars were in canvas sacks stored in a crevice in that cave where you were held hostage. The stampings on the metal bars meant nothing to me, except those which told the weight in ounces. I didn't know where it came from."

"But you knew it wasn't yours."

"In a mining town, silver and gold belongs to the man who finds it. I was the only one here, so, by custom, it is mine."

"That only applies to ore found in the earth."

Sandoval shrugged. "Who can argue over a fine point such as that?"

Charvein knew the man was only trying to justify his actions. If caught, he could always state it wasn't his job to go hunting for the owner. He was just sitting on the gold, waiting for the right person to show up and claim it.

"I used the assay office to melt the bars," Sandoval continued. "Formed clay molds and cast the gold into two thirty-pound clappers. I kept a few ingots to cut up and melt into small nuggets to trade for supplies when I went to town." He cast a look upward. "It was a terrible struggle trying to hang those heavy clappers in that bell. I had to rig a hoist."

Lucy had gone to the foot of the ladder and was looking up at the subject of discussion.

"Those clappers account for only about half of the total weight of the ingots," Charvein said.

"About twenty pounds I kept for expenses, as I said. The rest I melted. Tried to cast a small bell for the sanctuary." He shrugged. "But I failed. I am not a craftsman. I fashioned a simple cross of the remaining forty pounds. It is hidden inside the altar. The Christ child did not refuse the gift of gold from the Magi, so I pray He will accept mine."

Charvein didn't know whether this man was only pretending to be devout to justify his taking of another's

gold, or if he was really sincere. "You know I have to report this to the rightful owner who hired me to find it,"
Charvein said.

"Ah, Señor Charvein, you do not wear well the mask of
a self-righteous man. Remember the gospel story of the
Pharisee and the Publican? You do not want to cast your lot
with the Publican and be condemned by Jesus."

"Nothing self-righteous about being honest," Charvein
said.

"We are a long way from Virginia City, señor," Sandoval
reminded him. "And we have no real reason to think we'll
live to get back there."

Charvein took this as a veiled threat, whether or not
it was meant that way. As if to emphasize the truth of
Sandoval's words, two shots rang out close together and a
bullet came through the open doorway, smashing one of the
wine bottles holding a candle on the altar in the sanctuary.
The three of them jumped and moved quickly back to their
positions just inside the doorway.

"Men will do anything to possess gold," Sandoval said.
"Even my Spanish ancestor came across the ocean in search
of it, killed many of my Indian ancestors and took it."

"Those men over there have no knowledge of the clappers," Charvein mused.

"*Verdad*. That's why we must defend this church. If they
get in, they could easily find it," Sandoval said.

"So this is our Alamo," Lucy said, eyes bright.

"Except the odds are a little more even," Charvein said,
hoping she was not reverting to imagining herself in some
sort of heroic setting. "Thousands of Mexican soldiers with
cannons would be a far different story."

Sandoval's words had planted the seed of an idea. "I said
we would wait until dark to see what develops." He looked
at each of them, and then at the long shadows stretching

down Center Street. "Probably two hours until dark this time of year."

"Sooner, tonight," Sandoval remarked, pointing at the bank of dark gray clouds sliding in from the west on a steady breeze.

"No blowing dust tonight?"

"Not tonight. The wind is high up, driving clouds across the mountains from the western sea, many miles away. The clouds will not bring water. It is not the right time of year."

"When night falls, we'll break the rungs from that ladder so they cannot climb to the belfry. Then we abandon this church. Instead of worrying about where they are in the dark, let them worry about where *we* are."

Lucy gave a slight shiver. "It's all so mysterious and dangerous."

"Deadly dangerous," Charvein emphasized. "This is no game of hide-and-seek, Lucy. Remember that."

"I'm not sure that is the best thing to do," Sandoval said.

"Do you have a better plan? You are part Indian. We're both wearing moccasins and can surprise them in the dark. If we keep our nerve, we can take them. Lucy can go back to your cave for ammunition if we need it. We would have all the advantage."

"Do you plan to kill them?" Lucy asked.

"If it comes to that, yes. We can't take chances. They've shown they mean to kill us. We'll give them every opportunity to surrender, but it'll be on our terms—*if* we can corner them. Not an easy thing to do."

Since Boyd and Rankin had the belfry under fire, Charvein, Sandoval, and Lucy stayed out of it for the rest of the afternoon. They took turns guarding the back door of the church that led out of the sanctuary, to be sure they weren't surprised.

The other two guarded the wide front doorway. Charvein saw some movement behind the broken window across
the street and wondered what his two enemies were doing
to pass the time. He couldn't imagine how Boyd and Rankin,
an ex-convict and an ex-lawman, could agree to work together. The threat of a common enemy? He pondered this.
More likely they'd fused Rankin's hatred of Sandoval and
Boyd's lust for gold. Something had brought Boyd back to
Lodestar, something had convinced him the gold was still
here and hadn't been discovered and hauled away by some
unknown thief. Charvein heard the mumble of voices from
across the street and wished he could become invisible in
order to eavesdrop on their conversation.

As time began to drag, he and Lucy and Sandoval
stopped talking among themselves. They consumed the
food and drank the wine Sandoval had brought and replen-
ished their canteens from the big, wicker-covered bottle.
The boost of energy provided by the nourishment gradually
wore off by sunset. Charvein wondered what food, if any,
the men over there had to eat. Hunger and thirst had to be
nagging at them by now.

Would sunset never come? Charvein fought drowsiness,
but dared not relax too much.

The sun finally died in a welter of reds and golds. Beyond the buildings, the sky flushed a spectacular rose, the
last rays reflecting airborne dust and the undersides of approaching clouds.

Shadows inked in the spaces between buildings, slowly
blurring their view of the street. Silence reigned.

Sandoval was watching the back door; Charvein looked
across at Lucy on the opposite side of the big open doorway. She was sagging with fatigue and boredom.

When it was almost too dark to see, Charvein crept over
and touched her shoulder. She jerked up. "Sshh!" he whis-

pered, and took her by the elbow to guide her quietly toward the sanctuary, where Sandoval looked up at their coming. "Time to go," Charvein said, sotto voce.

"Do we break the rungs of the ladder as we planned?"

Charvein shook his head. "Changed my mind. Too noisy. Besides, if they notice the newly destroyed ladder, they'll suspect there's something up above we don't want them to find. If they happen to climb up there, it's now too dark to notice the scuff marks on the clappers."

"Follow me," Sandoval said, gliding away into the deepening dusk and out the side door into the alleyway. The air hadn't cooled much, but the slight breeze felt fresher than the stifling interior of the church.

Sandoval's poncho sagged with extra boxes of cartridges carried in the inside pockets, so he cinched it around him with a piece of rope to keep the garment from swinging and banging against his body.

The trio made their way along the alley to the lower end of town, moving carefully in the dark to avoid making noise. Two hundred yards from the church, Sandoval held up his hand and they halted. "Something moving there," he whispered. He took a few steps forward. "Ahh, only Boyd's mules," Sandoval said. "Grazing with my livestock."

Charvein heard and saw nothing. Indian instincts? Then a slight shift in the breeze brought the faint sound of teeth ripping at the sparse clumps of grass. And he caught a slight whiff of the animals.

"Are your weapons fully loaded?" Charvein asked.

They checked their guns. Sandoval thrust a few more .44 rimfire cartridges into the tubular magazine of his old Henry. Charvein and Lucy used the same .45s in their Colts. Charvein took the box from Sandoval, opened it, and roughly divided the remaining loose cartridges between them. Lucy dropped hers into the pocket of her dress.

Before they began stalking the two men, Charvein tried to think of some plausible errand for Lucy so she wouldn't suspect she was being sent out of danger. Each of them had a canteen, they'd already eaten, and they had loaded guns. Perhaps he could assign her to return to the cavern and lure the animals closer with some grain so she could unsaddle Boyd's mules. But that would be chancy in the dark. She was bound to make some noise doing it, and he wasn't too sure how familiar she was with managing strange livestock.

He decided to use her as a lookout. She could be their backup if they ran into serious trouble. "Let's go. Lucy, stay down here near the end of the street. Sandoval and I'll swing around behind the building where those men were hiding. I was going to suggest you could get hold of those animals, but don't bother with that; they won't wander off. Just stay close to the street and watch and listen." The three walked between the buildings from the alley into the main street. "You hear shooting, don't come near. If they get us, I don't want them getting you, too. Take to the cavern, where you can hide and defend yourself, if need be. If we come out on top, one or both of us will meet you right here near this striped barber pole. Keep your gun handy."

"I will."

"Feel like a little blind hunting, amigo?"

Sandoval muttered his assent.

"Then, let's go."

"Oh!" Lucy gasped when they were all startled by a flicker of lightning in the distance. They paused, looking toward the northwestern sky. A few seconds later, it came again, backlighting a heavy, ragged cloud formation. There was no following rumble of thunder.

"Heat lightning," Sandoval said. "No rain for us in those clouds. They are miles away."

After many days of blistering sun and blowing dust, Charvein welcomed even a suggestion of possible moisture.

But they had other things to think about now, and he gave Lucy's hand a reassuring squeeze before he and Sandoval moved off diagonally across the street in the blackness and then circled back toward the church. They walked in the dirt street so their footfalls wouldn't be heard on the hollow boardwalk. The solid blanket of cloud over the moon ensured they couldn't be seen. Sandoval, intimately familiar with the town, was able to navigate with confidence in complete darkness. Charvein wasn't convinced the man didn't have the night vision of a cat.

They were less than fifty yards from the front of the church when torchlight suddenly outlined the big doorway from within. Boyd and Rankin had wasted no time. They'd also waited for dark before moving in for an attack. The light flickered from window to window. Unintelligible conversation, then angry curses came to their ears on the light breeze. The sweat on Charvein's skin felt cool under his shirt. Boyd and Rankin had discovered them gone and now it was their turn to worry, Charvein thought, grimly.

Then he realized that the light came not from a torch but from two candles—probably the candles they'd found on the altar.

He and Sandoval crouched in the darkness, waiting, watching. Slowly, the belfry began to lighten and the bell come into view as one of the men climbed the ladder. Charvein stood, extended his gun, and steadied his arm against a porch post. He sighted carefully on the bell, cocked his Colt, and fired once, then again, quickly.

"Son of a bitch!" The candle went out and there was a thumping noise of something falling or being dropped.

"You tickled his funny bone, señor."

"Or something."

"He won't climb back into the bell tower with a light."

"And without a light he won't see the marks of the exposed gold."

Jumbled voices emanated from the church. What would be their next move? They didn't have to wait long to find out. The other candle went out and all was silent for the space of five heartbeats. Then boots thumped hollowly on the floor and a flash of heat lightning showed a glimpse of two men dashing out the front door. The Colt and the Henry roared as one, but the figures were moving too fast, and the darkness was too profound.

"Damn!" A cold knot formed in Charvein's stomach. The two men on the loose were more manhunters than he and Sandoval, who now had to stay on the move. He touched Sandoval's arm. *"Vamanos!"*

They faded down the street the way they'd come. Charvein didn't want either Boyd or Rankin to stumble upon Lucy by herself. Reluctant as he was to let her join them, he now had no choice. With that pair roaming the streets, the three of them had to stick together. The deadly stalking game had begun.

TWENTY-TWO

Even without blowing dust to obscure the atmosphere, Charvein was amazed at the blackness of the night. Cloud covered moon and stars. He thought the white stripes of the barber pole would be at least dimly visible. They were not.

"Where's that damned barbershop?" he whispered to Sandoval, hesitating, thinking they'd retreated far enough. Without answering, Sandoval went ahead. Twenty paces later they stumbled against the raised boardwalk and Charvein vaguely picked out the striped pole. "Lucy!" he hissed.

"Here!" came a subdued voice to his right.

"We flushed them out of the church."

"I think they headed toward the other end of town," Sandoval said.

"I believe it's better we hole up and not move around," Charvein said. "Pick them off if they come near us."

"Yes. It is a quiet night. We can hear them moving," Sandoval agreed. "I know a good place near the middle of town. Follow me."

He padded away with Lucy following and Charvein last.

They didn't speak. Charvein wondered if they were making any sound that could be heard more than a few yards away. He didn't know where Sandoval was going, but they seemed to take a long time getting there. Distances were distorted in the darkness.

Finally, Sandoval crept up to a small building that stood on a corner. He eased aside the door that had only one hinge, and the others followed him inside.

After a few seconds of feeling their way around, Charvein thought the layout was familiar, judging by the outlines of the windows briefly lit up by the lightning. "This is the assay office."

"*Sí.* We can defend it from two sides."

Charvein formed a mental picture of the two-room building, office in front and workroom and smelter in an adjacent rear room. "This is where we found the trapdoor to the tunnel," he whispered to Lucy.

"Yes. It saved us," she replied quietly. There was no tremor in her voice. Apparently, she felt safer in the presence of Charvein and Sandoval. He must always act as if he had supreme confidence they'd come out of this alive.

"We must sit very still and not talk," Sandoval whispered. "Sounds can be heard very far on a night like this."

Charvein felt his way to an open side window. "Anybody comes up this side street gets a bullet," Charvein said, going to one knee. "Lucy, you guard the back door to the alley. Sandoval will watch the main street," he added at the scuffing of a chair being moved to the front window.

Lucy stepped around the counter toward the back room, her feet crunching on broken glass.

They sat silently at their posts, Charvein recalling the lucky escape when he and Lucy had fled down the tunnel that led to the bank. The man who'd fired blindly at them in the dark was long gone, but Boyd had been with them and knew about the tunnel. He wondered why Sandoval had chosen this particular building to make their stand. Was it because of the tunnel? Not likely. Probably because the assay office stood in the middle of the long street, increasing the likelihood Boyd and Rankin would pass nearby, regardless from which direction they came.

They heard and saw nothing for a long time. Probably really only ten or fifteen minutes, Charvein guessed. But patience was more in Sandoval's line.

"I hope they haven't found those animals," Charvein whispered. "Or they could ride right out of here. Probably not a bad thing," he added, thinking of avoiding any violent conflict while Lucy was here.

"They will not leave," Sandoval replied, shifting his position slightly. "Rankin still wants to kill me. Even if they find the mules, they will not ride out until I am dead."

"And Boyd won't be satisfied until he finds the gold," Charvein said.

"One is a rapist and murderer, and the other a convicted robber. Either of them will kill. Boyd ambushed you on your ride to Lodestar," Sandoval reminded him.

"That's so," Charvein murmured. "We are dealing with two dangerous men who will stop at nothing to get what they want—gold and revenge." He spoke only to hear the whispered sound of his own voice beating back the suffocating silence. Except for the taste of dust, he almost preferred the roar of the night wind to this deafening stillness.

He looked out the window at the flicker of heat lightning. It seemed no closer than before. Maybe the cloud mass was passing off to the north. Another flash from the heavens. This time, instead of just blinking off and on behind the clouds, it branched out in a crazy pattern like ice cracking, spiking across the distant horizon. It was an entertaining, silent light show without thunder or threat of rain.

He thrust his head out the open window to smell air fresher than the musty odor in the room. Even the gentle breeze had died. What a contrast to the roaring winds of other nights. He'd never experienced a night as dark or silent. He could almost hear his own heart beat. His breathing seemed loud in his ears, as if it could be heard thirty yards away. He found himself wanting to hold his breath for fear of being heard. He knew that no living creature the size of a man could be anywhere close and be so silent. Yet, he'd been told Apaches had that ability. But these were two white men. He guessed they were some distance away, possibly searching the town, systematically, from one end to the other.

He heard Sandoval stir and slide out of his chair. Charvein crept to his side.

"Something out there," Sandoval whispered, close to his ear.

Charvein strained his eyes and ears but could detect nothing. He held his breath, the deathly silence unbearable. Yet he knew Sandoval had the senses of a cougar. He wondered if the man's nose was as keen as his hearing or sight. Somehow, he'd been able to find Charvein on the edge of town that terrible night when he'd nearly died in the dust storm.

Suddenly, about forty yards away, he saw a point of light wink on, then disappear. "There!" But he knew Sandoval had seen it before he did. A match? A candle being snuffed?

Sandoval yanked the Henry to his shoulder, worked the lever, and fired. Before the roar died away, he was pumping another round into the chamber, and Charvein was blasting away in the general direction of the vanished speck of light.

They paused, and there was no sound. The night seemed as empty as before.

"Reckon we hit anything?" Charvein whispered. He sensed Lucy's excited breathing at his shoulder. "Stay down," he said. "They might shoot back."

She groaned an inarticulate reply.

Suddenly he heard a metallic clatter. The light appeared again, this time stronger, or closer. It was moving fast. Both men fired, but the light swung in a wide arc and came hurtling toward them like a shooting star.

"Down!" He threw Lucy down, while Sandoval jerked away to the other side. The window shattered and the lantern crashed against the wooden counter behind them, spewing flaming coal oil on the floor.

"Oh, my God!" she screamed.

Flames had splashed Sandoval's poncho, and Charvein tackled him, smothering the fire before the flames could burn him through the woven cloth.

"I'm okay," Sandoval gasped, pulling the smoking poncho off over his head.

Lucy was cowering in the corner, pistol in one hand, eyes wide in the light of the flames that were licking up the counter and spreading across the floor.

"Stay down!" Charvein yelled. "Don't make a target." The sudden brightness had blinded him, and he fired through the window with little hope of hitting anyone. He saw muzzle flashes from outside, and bullets smashed the remaining shards of glass that clung to the sash. By the time he and Sandoval returned fire, the flashes had moved, coming closer.

The fire was spreading rapidly, flames hungrily licking up the walls, consuming the dry wood.

A bullet smashed the side window where Charvein had kept watch.

"They're on two sides."

"They'll gun us down as soon as we run out," Charvein said, firing two shots out the front as he moved Lucy back behind the counter into the next room.

"We can't stay here and burn!" Lucy's voice was shrill.

Sandoval was already at work tugging at the iron ring recessed into the floor.

Dry wood crackled in the flames.

Sandoval heaved up the trapdoor and laid it back on the floor.

"Oh, no! Not again!" Lucy wailed softly, her eyes on the yawning black hole. "Do we have to?"

"Unless we want to run out, night-blind, and shoot it out," Charvein said. "You two go down first." He knew he was the best shot. "I'll be rear guard. Hurry!" he added as the heat became intense.

Whoosh! The flames rushed across the ceiling, invading the back room. The tinder-dry building was nearly engulfed. Oxygen was being sucked out of the air.

Sandoval descended the ladder, then helped Lucy down. Crouching with his Colt at hip level, Charvein fired a shot out of each window. He tried once more, but the hammer clicked on a spent shell. He grabbed the trapdoor and tilted it up, stepping into the hole and letting the heavy door down overhead, suddenly shutting out the roar and heat and light. Even if the town had been full of people, there was no means of fighting this fire, what with the town pumps rusted. Luckily, there was absolutely no breeze tonight.

The tunnel was musty, hot, and black as the inside of a boot.

"Got any matches?" Marc asked.

"Sí."

"Strike one and let's get moving."

The match flared in a sharp smell of sulfur. Sandoval led the way. The air was stuffy but cooler.

The match burned out in a matter of seconds. "No need for light," Sandoval said. "I know this tunnel. There is a candle stashed at the far end."

This time Charvein traversed the tunnel with no uncertainty about where it would lead. He knew it terminated beneath the bank. He thought of the men behind them who'd fired the assay office in a vain attempt to smoke them out. Boyd knew of the tunnel, but he and Rankin had cut themselves off from it until the embers cooled the next day. By then, Lodestar might be no more—the old mining town reduced to a smoking ruin. Could the blaze become hot enough, Charvein wondered, to roast them underground, as in a fire pit?

They reached the end, and Sandoval struck another match to light their steps over and around the pile of lumber that was the collapsed stairs. He located his thick candle and lighted it. The steady, warm glow that suffused their faces was a relief from the dark.

"I have put in many hours over the past year extending this tunnel," Sandoval said, holding up the candle. See those wood planks? I stood them on end to block the tunnel I have dug beyond this point."

"Why dig farther?" Charvein asked.

"I was looking for ways to fill many lonely hours," Sandoval said and shrugged. "I wanted to see if I could bring it up under San Juan church."

"How far does it go?" Lucy asked.

Sandoval turned toward them, hooded eyes looking sinister in the candlelight. "I measured above, and then measured below as I dug, using a compass to maintain direction. I'm certain the end of the tunnel is directly beneath the sacristy."

"You haven't dug upward to find out?"

He shook his head. "I was planning to, but suddenly, I had many visitors in town and had to stop."

"I wonder if Boyd knows this tunnel comes up in the bank," Charvein said to Lucy.

"I'm sure they know. They searched all the buildings, and we left many marks in the dust near the vault," she replied.

"Let's take a look at the rest of your tunnel," Charvein said. "Maybe we can find a safer way out."

Sandoval handed the candle to Lucy and thrust the upright planks aside far enough for them to squeeze through.

The smell of fresh, dry dirt assailed them as they entered. Their feet trod the softer, unpacked dirt. The tunnel was narrower and not shored up. Charvein began to feel a prickly claustrophobia.

The tunnel was only thirty paces long. A shovel was thrust into the face of the drift, and a wheelbarrow half-full of dirt rested just below where Sandoval had interrupted his labor.

The candle was beginning to burn low with lack of oxygen.

"How far below ground are we?" Charvein asked.

"No more than three feet."

"And you say the church is just overhead?"

"I believe it is."

"How did you plan to break through the floor of the church?" Charvein was perspiring heavily from the closeness of the air.

"I was going to rip up the floor from above and see if I could break through into this tunnel."

"We should probably go back and climb out through the bank," Lucy said hesitantly, passing a delicate, grimy hand over her forehead.

"Too much chance Boyd and Rankin are waiting to gun us down," Charvein said. "The more I think about it, the more I can see that was their plan all along—drive us down into the tunnel and wait for us to come out the other end, like prairie dogs."

Lucy gave a slight shiver. Even in the soft, yellow light, her face had taken on a pallid hue.

Charvein made a quick decision. "Let's see what's right up above. Are we agreed?" He glanced at them. "Can't hurt anything. We might still have to wind up going back."

"Then, let me do it," Sandoval said. "I know what this soil will take. If you hit it wrong with the shovel, it could cave in and bury us."

This was not what Charvein wanted to hear. He took Lucy's arm and retreated about ten steps, leaving the candle with Sandoval.

Sandoval took the long-handled shovel and gently probed overhead. Dry dirt pattered down, and he stopped to move the candle out of the way. Slowly, gently, he cut with the point of the shovel, standing back to let the ceiling crumble, a little at a time, filling the wheelbarrow.

Charvein stood in the dark, holding Lucy's hand.

Sandoval paused, breathing heavily, and took the candle, holding it high to inspect his work.

Charvein felt Lucy's free hand touch his arm. "Whatever happens," she said softly, "I want you to know that I appreciate everything you've done for me."

"*De nada,*" he said, taking refuge in Spanish from his slight embarrassment.

"I feel very safe when I'm with you."

"Good." It was a feeling he'd gone out of his way to engender. He wondered if he'd have treated her the same if she'd been an ugly, sharp-tongued shrew. Probably not. As a forty-year-old bachelor, he'd lived most of his life in a male world and realized he was seriously lacking in social skills.

"Lucy, I . . ."

"Ahh! That's it!" came a low cry from Sandoval, who stepped back, spitting the dirt out of his mouth. "Busted through."

Charvein and Lucy came forward and looked at the ceiling where Sandoval was holding up the thick candle.

"I don't see the floor of the church."

"I did not measure it right," Sandoval said.

"Ain't nothing up there but sky," Charvein said. "I just saw a flicker of lightning. He could smell the rush of fresh air that came down the hole. "Hell, that's even better. Now we can get out without being seen. Stand on that pile of dirt in the wheelbarrow, and I'll boost you up," he said to Sandoval.

"One moment, señor. There is something I must take with me."

"What's that?"

"You will see. It's stored in the bigger tunnel. Come and help me carry it." He took the candle, squeezed past them, and headed back the way they'd come.

Charvein followed. What could this be?

Sandoval shoved aside the upright planks that partially divided the tunnels. Being careful of rusty nails in the scrap lumber, he stooped and shifted several of the splintered boards and pieces of rotted stairs that lay piled here and there.

"Hold the candle." He handed it back to Charvein, squatted by four small, wooden cases stacked on the floor next to the wall. Lifting the lid on the top one, he pulled back a layer of cotton padding. Candlelight reflected from red paper-wrapped cylinders—row upon row of dynamite sticks neatly packed to the top of the box.

TWENTY-THREE

"Whew!" Charvein gave a low whistle. "You're full of surprises. Where did this come from?"

"I found it stored in a tool shed with drill bits and shovels, near one of the mines," Sandoval replied. "These are my *diablos rojos*—my little red devils. I used them only to move boulders and old rusty machinery—until now." His hooded eyes showed a hint of mirth. "I must store them out of the heat to keep them from becoming very nervous and sweating nitro. It's not really cool down here, but better than up there." He jerked a thumb upward. He picked out four sticks and handed them to Charvein. "They're dry so they should be safe enough. But handle them *con cuidado*. Gently.

"I've already inserted a blasting cap into the end of each stick," Sandoval said. "I crimp the cap around each fuse as I insert it." He took up one of the sticks, shoved in the end of the fuse, then bit down on it.

Charvein grimaced, feeling sweat pop out on his forehead. "Careful!" he whispered. Crimping fulminate-ofmercury caps like this, with the teeth, was a very dangerous procedure. One bite too close to the dynamite and they could all be part of a large hole in the ground.

"Do not worry. I have done this many times, and I am very good at it." Sandoval spoke with confidence.

They spent another ten minutes cutting and inserting fuses, Sandoval biting at a precise spot on each to crimp the cap around the fuse.

"I wish we had a punk or a cigar for a glowing fire to light these when we need them," Charvein said.

"That would be best," Sandoval agreed. "But we must use what we have—matches and candle. Thank God the wind is nearly calm."

Charvein could never quite fathom the thinking of this recluse. But it was always logical and practical, if not predictable.

"I hope the fire from the assay office hasn't spread," Charvein said, stuffing his pockets with several sticks.

"My poncho had extra pockets," Sandoval said with regret. The smoldering garment had been left in the burning assay office.

"Did you leave anything in your poncho?" Charvein asked.

A strange look came over Sandoval's face, and he paused in handing out the sticks. "Half a box of .44 rimfires for my Henry. I was in a hurry."

"I'm sure the fire has set them off by now. We wouldn't hear 'em from down here, but I'll bet Boyd and Rankin were ducking. Wish I'd seen their reaction. They must think we're supernatural if we could stay inside that inferno and still keep shooting."

"We are fireproof," Sandoval said, a trace of smile on his thin lips. "And, with these little red devils, we will surely make them believe we are from the depths of hell."

Charvein turned to Lucy. "You have only one pocket in that dress?"

"Yes, but it's a deep one."

"Here." He slid eight dynamite sticks into the pocket. The fuses dangled out of the top like fringe. She avoided touching them, as if her pocket were full of scorpions.

"*Bastante*," Sandoval said, closing the lid of the empty box. "There is another full case here, but if this won't hold them at bay, then we are doomed anyway."

"We're now walking bombs," Charvein said, a chill going up his spine at the thought of the sticks detonating. "Let's go." He was anxious to get above ground to see if the whole town was ablaze and to find their two antagonists.

They divided the wooden matches so each had eight. Sandoval took the candle and the empty dynamite box and led them back to the hole he'd knocked in the ceiling. The two men walked slightly bent over through the narrow, low portion of the tunnel he'd dug.

"Let me go first," Charvein said, upending the dynamite box to serve as a stool. He drew his Colt and carefully stepped up, extending his arms over his head through the narrow hole, then straightened up. His eyes were just above ground level.

An unnatural glow lighted the town. He wiggled his elbows over the rim and muscled his body upward, praying that neither Rankin nor Boyd had their sights trained on the hole. He crawled out and lay flat on his stomach, while his eyes adjusted to the glare of flames some distance off. Where was he? In spite of Sandoval's calculations, the tunnel had veered off at an oblique angle, and Charvein found himself twenty feet from the rear of the church, toward the alley.

He turned a half circle and saw an eight-foot fence with several of its vertical palings missing. The light of the ap-

proaching flames shone through the fence like a candle
from inside a gap-toothed jack-o'-lantern. Through one of
the gaps, Charvein could just make out the fire at the assay
office declining as the building fell in on itself in a shower
of sparks. But flying sparks had ignited the next two buildings and a wave of flames slowly moved toward them.

Scanning a full circle, Charvein saw no sign of Boyd or
Rankin. He holstered his gun, crawled back to the hole, and
thrust an arm down inside. "Give me your hand." Up came
the Henry rifle followed by two lean, muscular arms. Charvein squatted, locked onto the wrists, and heaved the lithe
man upward to the surface.

And lastly came Lucy, brushing dirt out of her hair and
eyes.

"I slanted off course with that tunnel," Sandoval muttered, looking around.

"Probably just as well, since we couldn't have busted
through the church floor," Charvein said. He saw Sandoval
looking warily around. "No sign of them," he added.

The approaching fire crackled as it devoured the buildings. They could feel the heat and see sparks showering red
against the black sky.

"I always feared this town would catch fire by lightning
or some accident," Sandoval said. "Never thought anyone
would do it on purpose. It's so dry, it will all burn down."

"But only one side of the street," Charvein said. "Good
thing the night wind isn't blowing, or the whole town would
be alight by now."

A rifle shot blasted from the darkness.

"Oh!" Lucy staggered and would have fallen except for
Charvein, who was there to catch her before she hit the
ground. He swiftly laid her down next to the fence.

Sandoval was on his belly, jacking a round into the
chamber.

Another bullet slammed into the fence over their heads. Sandoval fired back at the muzzle flash coming from behind the church.

"Lucy, you hit bad?" Charvein had his Colt out and fired once.

Sandoval fired again and was rewarded with someone shouting a curse.

"My leg," she gasped, pulling at the torn hem of her dress.

"Let's get you to cover," he said, carrying her around the street end of the fence. His stomach had a fist-size ball in it as he examined her wounded leg. In the glare he saw a neat, round hole in the fleshy part of her left calf, about an inch from the outer edge. He felt beneath and his fingers came away bloody from the exit wound. "Bullet went through. Good." Some bleeding, but not profuse. Apparently clipped part of the muscle, but not an artery. Aloud, he said, "We'll bind this up and have you good as new in no time." He was vastly relieved and tried to make light of it, but he knew it probably hurt like hell and would pain her even worse later.

"Can you stand or walk?" he asked.

She nodded, biting her lip.

More firing from beyond the fence.

Charvein helped her to her feet, and she took a couple of tentative steps, leaning on him. He eased her back to the ground. "I'll be back in a minute. Got to help Sandoval."

"I dropped my Colt when I was hit," she said.

"No matter. Take one of those dynamite sticks and a match and be ready." He sensed she was deathly afraid but was trying desperately not to show it.

He pulled his Colt and sprinted to the end of the fence, then got down and bellied around to avoid being backlit by the fire.

Sandoval lay prone in the shadow, firing his Henry at some unseen target in the alley behind the church.

"Can you see them?"

"Only muzzle flashes."

"There!" Charvein snapped off a shot at a dim figure darting sideways toward a rain barrel.

"How's Lucy?" Sandoval whispered.

"Minor calf wound. She'll be all right, but we have to get those two or we'll all be in a fix. Get close enough, we can use the dynamite."

"Not yet. That's our ace in the hole. We must be sure." He aimed the Henry and squeezed the trigger. The hammer fell with a dull click.

"Empty." He laid the rifle down and crawled back a few feet into the deeper shadow of the fence. "That's all I have. Extras were in my poncho."

"Wait." Charvein bellied toward the spot where Lucy was hit. Feeling around, he finally touched the pistol she'd dropped.

Scuttling back, he handed over the Colt. "It's loaded, and here're a few of my spare shells. Lucy still has seven or eight in her pocket."

"*Bueno!* Now I have two pistols."

Two shots blasted from behind the church, slugs slamming into the fence behind them.

Sandoval fired back at the flashes.

Five or six shots exploded in a sudden roar, kicking up dirt and gravel in front of them.

"Uh!" Charvein gasped as a fragment of lead ricocheted and burned the edge of his scalp at the hairline. It felt like a bee sting; warm blood trickled down his forehead. He untied his bandanna and dabbed at it.

The roar of gunfire ceased.

"They're covering their retreat into the back door of the church," Sandoval said. "I saw them run inside. They're barricaded now."

For a minute all was quiet, save the crackling of approaching flames.

"They've expended a lot of ammunition," Charvein said. "Do you reckon they've run out?"

"Not yet," Sandoval said. "They likely carried enough cartridges that would fit into their belt loops. But even if those were full, a belt does not carry more than thirty-five or so."

Charvein tried to recall approximately how many shots he'd heard fired that day. "They can't have many left. Maybe saving the last few for one final defense—or attack."

"Which do you think?"

"What?" Charvein said.

"Attack or defense?"

"Wish I knew," Charvein said. "All I know is they're in there, and we're out here. We've just switched positions from earlier. But I think they'll try to end this soon."

"*Creo que sí,*" Sandoval muttered. "I believe you're right."

"But we have this," Charvein said, holding up a stick of dynamite.

"We must save that as a last resort," Sandoval said.

"What do you think this is, if not a last resort? If we expose ourselves, or try to rush them, we could both be killed."

Sandoval was silent for a moment. "It would be a sacrilege to blow up the church."

"I don't know much about the beliefs of the Catholic faith, but I've been told that if the Eucharist is not present, then it's just a building; there's nothing holy about it."

"*Verdad.* The body of Christ is not there."

Silence again.

Charvein glanced upward. Showers of sparks patterned the blackness and rained down as the fire approached.

"I'm going to check on Lucy. We have to move from here soon."

"Bring all her dynamite here," Sandoval said.

Charvein loped around the end of the fence, drawing no fire. He knew the two men were likely watching from one of the stained glass windows in this side of the church, but he was now convinced they were saving their ammunition.

He squinted in the brightness of the flames that were consuming the next building, less than ninety feet away. The heat was becoming intense.

Lucy was stretched out on her side at the base of the fence, unconscious. He turned her faceup. Taking up the canteen that lay beside her, he poured water into his hand and wiped her warm face. The second time he did it, her eyes fluttered open. "My leg," she gasped.

He took a quick look. It was no worse than before. Some blood had crusted around the wound. "We'll fix it," he assured her. She must have fainted from the shock, or fear, or a combination of things. He could hardly blame her. And the worst was yet to come. "Can you stand up?" He could have easily carried her, but he hoped she'd make the effort on her own.

"I'll try."

He slid an arm under and raised her to a sitting position. "I need your dynamite," he said, helping himself to the sticks that barely protruded from her front pocket. He shoved them inside his shirt. "Okay, now!" She pushed erect, leaning heavily on him.

"Around the back edge of the fence, away from the fire and into the alley." He thought this the safest course to avoid gunshots from the church.

Once in the cooler darkness away from the bright flames, she said, "Felt a little dizzy for a minute, but I'm okay now."

He kept walking with his arm around her; she hobbled

along, seemingly able to bear a little more of her own weight.

"Where we going?"

"Far away from the fire, where it's safe," he said, neglecting to add that he wanted her out of range of the battle.

Beyond the outhouses and storage sheds of the alley, they approached open land leading to the edge of the playa. They stopped, and he eased her to the ground. "Wait here, no matter what you hear." He slipped the canteen from his shoulder. "Have a good drink of water and rest. Gather your strength. Sandoval and I are going to deal with Boyd and Rankin, who're holed up in the church. This fight will end very shortly."

"Oh, be careful," she whispered. "Don't take any chances."

"You can bet on it," he said, with all the confidence he could muster. "I'll be back." With that he turned and loped away, Colt in hand.

Creeping along the edge of the fence, he was surprised at how much easier he could see everything by the firelight. He found Sandoval where he'd left him. They were both within eyeshot of the church's side windows. The bottoms of the stained glass were about six feet above the floor inside the church. If Rankin and Boyd were to shoot from one of the windows, they'd have to find something to stand on.

"Here's the dynamite."

Sandoval bundled nine sticks together and tied them with a strip of cloth torn from his shirttail. Then he did the same with a second bundle of ten. He refashioned the fuses, twisting them together to form one fuse for each of the bundles. Not being used to handling such destructive power, Charvein felt a prickle of chill run up his arms and back.

"We've been on the defensive most of the day," Charvein said. "Protecting the girl and all. They probably feel safe inside that stone church. Not likely it'll even catch fire. And it'll stop bullets. They won't be expecting us to suddenly go on the offensive." He couldn't believe his own words. He was suggesting they attack the two men who were forted up and ready for them.

Sandoval silently handed him one of the bundles of dynamite. "You have matches?"

"Yes."

"The big front doors of the church are broken and will not close," Sandoval said.

Charvein nodded, recalling the wide entrance where the arched double doors were jammed open.

"We will both approach the front and try to take them with guns first."

"Right." Charvein thumbed open the loading gate of his Colt, half cocked the weapon, and turned the cylinder until he found and punched out two empty shells. Replacing them with two cartridges from his belt left him with only eight. He doubted he'd have time to reload once the ball opened. His heart rate quickened.

There was a quiet clicking as Sandoval turned the cylinders of each of his weapons. He snapped the loading gates shut, then rose to his feet, shoving the bundle of dynamite under his shirt.

Charvein did the same, wondering if he would have any conscious realization—even for a split second—should a bullet strike that bundle.

TWENTY-FOUR

"Ready?"

Charvein nodded. "As we approach the front, I doubt they'll be waiting just inside the doorway."

"In case they're watching, we must confuse them by circling the church and approaching from the other side," Sandoval said.

They padded silently along the fence to the alley and into the darkness at the back of the church, then around behind some outbuildings, where they paused for a good five minutes.

"In case they saw us, we'll let them wonder where we've gone," Charvein said, glancing at the fire. Its flames leapt fifty feet into the air as it roared toward them, devouring the dry buildings. The light was probably brightening the inside like a rising sun through the stained glass windows. That could both help and hurt.

They crept along the dark side of the church below the tall windows and neared the front. Charvein whispered to

Sandoval that they should leave the dynamite bundles just outside the doorway.

Sandoval leaned over to set his bundle down. From behind him, Charvein caught a slight movement inside the doorway. He shoved Sandoval aside at the instant a knife blade flashed in the firelight. The arm holding it banged across Sandoval's collarbone, and the knife clattered onto the stone steps. Charvein stumbled to one side and fired— too late. He caught a glimpse of Rankin limping into the deep shadows toward the confessional.

Charvein fired again, grabbing Sandoval by the shirt and pulling him back. But no return fire came from inside the church. Maybe Boyd and Rankin were nearly out of ammunition.

"You okay?"

"*Sí.*"

Both men bellied inside the doorway, guns in hands.

The outside fire lit the biblical figures of the saints in the stained glass windows and cast a blur of multicolored light across the rows of empty pews. Charvein rose above the back of the last pew in time to see Boyd dashing away along the side aisle toward the sanctuary. Charvein fired twice, the confined blasts deafening. He saw Boyd plunge forward but couldn't tell if he was hit or just diving for cover.

He edged toward Sandoval, who was scuffing along the floor several yards away. "You take Rankin—back by the confessional. I'll go for Boyd. He ran up front."

Sandoval nodded, his bronze face even darker in the tempered light through the stained glass.

Ducking below the level of the pews, Charvein scuttled forward along the left side aisle. He was nearly past the front pew when a flash lashed out from behind the pulpit a few feet away. The sagging wooden Communion rail stopped the slug. He slid behind the partial protection of the posts that remained in the ruined railing. He strained to hear Boyd moving, but only his own harsh breathing and thumping heart resounded in his ears.

He sensed movement nearby and fired. But it was like shooting at a phantom—never really there. Two return shots came fast, the blasts echoing off the semicircular wall of the sanctuary. The second shot tore splinters that raked across Charvein's neck. He felt a sting and then warm blood flowing inside his collar. Two near misses—he was running out of chances and felt his luck changing for the worse. Without a human target, he fired blindly again toward the pulpit. These two were as elusive as hummingbirds, as insubstantial as fog. How many shots did he have left? None. The hammer fell with a dull click. He crawled between the two front pews and reloaded, more by feel than sight.

As he snapped the loading gate shut, Sandoval's voice came from the back of the church. "Marc!" Charvein had never heard this tone and knew it was trouble. He crawled out and dashed along the aisle toward the rear. Shots blasted from front and rear, and a slug whined off the stone floor near his foot. He ignored it, sprinting even faster.

"Watch out!" Sandoval cried. Charvein didn't see the danger, but he dove to the floor and slid on his belly; a shot hit one of the Stations of the Cross on the wall just over his head. He looked for muzzle flashes, since the outside firelight wasn't reliable. He saw Sandoval crawling toward him, a dark stain on the floor behind.

Charvein shot twice—a fast covering fire until he could grab his friend and drag him behind a pew. "You hit bad?"

"No," he gasped. "Left arm. High up."

Charvein sensed movement by the wall near the confessional and fired in the general direction. His ears rang with the explosions, and he was so deafened, he couldn't tell how loud he was talking. He put his mouth near Sandoval's

ear. "Quick! Out the front." The two men scrambled toward
the outline of the big door. Slugs zinged off the stone walls.

They tumbled off the outside steps, away from the doorway, and Sandoval groaned as he landed on his wounded
arm.

Something poked Charvein's ribs. He groped to pitch it
aside, but his hand encountered one of the two bundles of
dynamite. He felt for the second bundle.

"Here!" He holstered his Colt and fumbled for a match
in his vest pocket.

"Let's go!" Rankin yelled. "We got 'em on the run!"

A figure appeared at the door, but Sandoval's Colt
roared.

"Shit!" Buck Rankin stumbled back inside.

"Something to think about, you wife-stealing bastard!"
Sandoval muttered through gritted teeth as he cocked his
weapon.

"You hit?" Boyd shouted.

"Naw! Damned greaser can't shoot. But I got a slug in
him," Rankin yelled.

Charvein struck the match on his belt buckle. Nothing.
He tried again, but in his haste he snapped the head off the
match. He groped for another one.

Sandoval, lying prone beside him, fired at the door, pin-
ning the pair inside. He cocked and aimed again. This time
the hammer fell with a sickening *click*. "Hurry, señor!" His
voice rasped with pain and urgency.

The match flared, and Charvein glanced aside from the
sudden glare. His hand trembled as he applied the flame to
the end of the fuse. It caught and sputtered, the fuse burning quicker than expected. He set the bundle of red sticks
down and touched the flame of the still-burning match to
the fuse of the second bundle.

Sandoval's hooded eyes went wide.

Charvein forced himself to wait until the sputtering, smoking fuses had roughly eight seconds to burn. Then he rose to his knees and hurled the first packet of red cylinders as far as he could through the open front door. The second bundle followed quickly.

"What the hell was that?" Boyd yelled.

"Under the pew! Get it out! Dynamite!" Rankin screamed in panic.

Charvein grabbed Sandoval by his good arm. "Run like hell!" He fired over his shoulder and saw Rankin stumble and fall out the doorway.

Sandoval was already on his feet and sprang ahead of Charvein, sprinting down the street away from the fire and the church.

A sudden surge of energy propelled Charvein after him, a clock ticking in his head.

They were less than fifty yards away when the dynamite blew.

TWENTY-FIVE

The church erupted in a thunderous roar of heat and light. The ground shook; they dove into the dirt. Stone fragments and shards of glass whizzed overhead. The concussion shattered the remaining windows in nearby buildings.

They crawled behind a horse trough and covered their heads. A hail of shattered rock and splintered boards rained down around them. Although semi-deafened, Charvein thought he heard the sound of a bell. He sneaked a look. The remaining pieces of wall and roof were collapsing in on one another, sliding and grinding to a halt as the wreckage settled into a pile.

They lay with arms over their heads for several more seconds. "Damn!" Charvein breathed as they got to their knees and then stood up.

Sandoval seemed to have forgotten the pain in his arm as they numbly walked toward the pile of smoking rubble that, a few minutes—and many years—before had been a church. Lighted by the nearby fire, a monstrous heap of rock and wood and tile lay smoking, clouds of dust rising.

The force of the explosion had blown down the nearest burning building, squelching the leaping flames. A few yards away, the wooden fence was ablaze, but the fire overall had lost its ferocity. The demolished church created a gap in the row of buildings, a firebreak against slowly advancing flames that had no wind to fan them. It appeared that the fire, lacking more fuel, and with fewer sparks flying upward, was destined to burn itself out in a few hours, confined to the destruction of five buildings.

"You reckon they're under there?" Charvein asked, finally, as they stood mesmerized by the smoldering heap before them. Debris was scattered out beyond the circle of light cast by the burning buildings.

Sandoval nodded, staring about him, a strained, vacant look on his dirt-streaked face. "Maybe in too many pieces to find." He made the sign of the cross. "A fitting burial—in the house of God with a gift of gold."

Until that moment, Charvein had forgotten about the gold. He saw no sign of the bell, but he recognized a corner of the belfry that had fallen straight down atop the roof and lay mostly buried.

"Let's find Lucy," Charvein said, still feeling stunned and hardly able to talk or think. "Then we'll get a look at that arm," he added, noting the drying blood streaking Sandoval's left sleeve.

They circled the rubble and started toward the alley. Before they'd gone thirty feet, Lucy came limping toward them. She came up and silently hugged Charvein. Then, turning toward Sandoval, she said, "You're hurt."

"No more than you," he replied, slipping his good arm around her shoulders.

"I feel fine," she said, belying her pale, pinched look. "I never knew dynamite had that much power."

"I used it all," Charvein said.

"Were those two men inside?"

"Yes."

"I'm so relieved the danger is past. My knees are weak," she said, sitting down on the ground. "But I almost feel sorry for them."

"They probably didn't know what hit them." Charvein was still trying to come down from the surge of energy and excitement; maybe later he'd feel something when it all began to sink in. For now, he had to assume Boyd and Rankin had died instantly in the blast. He recalled firing a parting shot at Rankin, who tried to bolt out the door just before the dynamite went off. The man had pitched forward, probably hit, so it was likely his body, or what was left of it, was under the rubble that covered the front steps.

"Let's go back to my cavern," Sandoval said. "I feel shaky."

Jarred out of his reverie, Charvein said, "We'll tend your arm, sleep, and then see about rounding up the livestock come daylight." He put out a hand and helped Lucy to her feet. "Lean on me," he said as they started down the street. "We're a sorry-looking bunch," he chuckled, touching the dried blood on his scalp wound. "Beat up, filthy, bloody, and exhausted."

"Hold that lantern closer, Lucy," Charvein said a half hour later, resting his unsteady hand on Sandoval's arm as he probed for the slug with the point of a thin-bladed knife. The lead wasn't deep.

"I think it bounced off the floor before it hit me," Sandoval said, grimacing.

"Sure looks that way," Charvein said, finally flicking the distorted bullet out into his hand. "You got any carbolic?"

"In that small chest by the wall, with some herbs I've

collected," he said, his face glistening with sweat in the yellow light.

Charvein doused the wound but left it unbandaged, then did the same for Lucy's calf muscle wound. He thought about trying to clean it completely with burning black powder but quickly gave up the idea. Years ago, during his time in the cavalry, he'd seen an arrow wound treated this way. The fletching had been broken off the protruding arrow, a groove cut along the top of the shaft, and black powder poured into the groove. At the instant one man touched a match to the powder, another drove the arrow on through the arm with the butt of his pistol. The powder flashed and burned as the arrow carried it through the wound. But this required skill and coordination to make it work properly. Lucy had no protruding arrow.

Charvein kept these thoughts to himself as he finished treating his two patients. "Sit there and rest while I get a fire going." He gathered a few dry sticks and broke them up. "Lucy, empty a canteen into this pot. We'll have a stew with beans, jerky, onions, and peppers, and anything else we can find."

He proceeded to build a small cooking fire inside the circle of stones at the entrance to the cavern. "I'll be right back," Charvein said, setting the blackened pot on the spider to boil. "Want to take a look around."

He slipped out through the screening mesquite bushes and walked a few yards into the blackness, sniffing the dry night air and listening to the silence. A faint odor of burning wood reached his nostrils, and a red glow was still visible a few hundred yards away in town. Why was he being so careful? Force of habit, he guessed. After all, the three of them were now the only human occupants of Lodestar, a town that had seen a lot more violence than this in its heyday.

His mind still worked on practicalities. The explosion
had likely spooked the animals even though they were far
enough away to be unharmed by it. They'd probably run off
toward the playa or the hills. But the sparse bunchgrass
near town would bring them back close enough to be
rounded up come daylight. He felt sure of it.

He returned to the cavern to find Lucy stirring a stew
that was giving off a wonderful aroma. Sandoval lit a second lantern and turned them both up bright so the inside of
the cavern took on a cheery aspect.

Shortly, the stew was done. They dished it up and folded
some tortillas to eat with it.

When they finished, the night was far gone. Charvein put
away the remaining stew, but even before he finished washing the dishes in a bucket of water, both Sandoval and Lucy
were sound asleep on their blankets. Fatigue was dragging
at him as well, and he had to keep moving, or he'd be asleep,
too. For some illogical reason, he felt someone needed to be
alert and on watch. And since he was the strongest and had
suffered only scratches, he elected himself.

Leaving one lantern lit and turned low, he reloaded his
Colt and stepped outside. The fire in town was dying, visible only as a red glow a quarter mile away. Turning east,
away from town, he saw a lighter gray streak along the
horizon. The earth was turning, coming around again to
bathe the battered old town in another day of light. Small,
nocturnal animals would cease hunting and seek their bur-
rows to sleep away the heat of the day. Nature continued her
cycles. He walked a few steps, listening to the peace and
silence.

Something bulked dimly before him—an old ore wagon
that had rolled its last mile. He put his hand on the seven-
foot-high rear wheel—a rusty iron band still holding the
massive rim and dried spokes together. Walking to the

front of the wagon, he sat down on the tilted tongue and leaned back against the rough timber of the box.

The light on the horizon slowly brightened into a rosy pink. He closed his eyes, the tension draining away. Was it possible for a man to sleep for two days without waking? He thought he could.

Bang!

The explosion jolted him awake. Something heavy fell against him, a sharp point raking his chest. He scrambled away, clawing at his holster. A man slumped over the wagon tongue, then rolled off to lie, faceup, on the ground. A red stain slowly spread on Buck Rankin's tattered white shirt.

Charvein, instantly alert, took in the scene. In full daylight thirty feet away, Lucy lowered the long Colt, a wisp of smoke curling from its muzzle. He swallowed twice, his mouth dry, but couldn't speak. His heart was racing.

"I woke up and came looking for you," she said in a steady voice. "Lucky I did."

"The blast didn't get him after all," Charvein said, hoarsely, glancing from her to the body on the ground. "And my shot missed, too."

Rankin's clothes were singed, his face bruised. Charvein stooped and checked to be sure the man was dead, then picked up the big Bowie knife that lay nearby. Only then did he realize he'd been cut. The left side of his shirt gaped open, and he was bleeding from a shallow slice down his rib cage. Blotting the wound with his shirt, he looked up and saw her standing with the heavy gun dangling from one hand. "I owe you my life," he said simply.

"I was here at the right time." She began to tremble, and the big pistol fell to the ground.

Charvein retrieved it.

"Are you all right?" she asked, her voice shaking.

"I'm okay. Just a scratch." He shoved the wide blade under his belt, thinking what might have been.

They turned toward the cavern. Sandoval came running toward them, Colt in hand.

"It's done," Charvein said, waving him to a halt. "She got Rankin just before he got me."

"What about Boyd?" Sandoval asked. "Did he also escape the church?"

"I don't think so. He was deeper inside. Rankin was the only one I saw get out the front door before the blast."

"We must be sure."

The three of them moved silently toward the ruins of the church, the two men with guns drawn, carefully surveying the town in the morning light.

Lucy limped on her wounded leg while Charvein supported her with his left arm around her waist. She was trembling.

"Are you all right?"

She nodded, blinking away tears. He guessed it was her instinctive action that had saved his life, but now the reaction was setting in.

They scoured the ground in a wide area around the pile of rubble.

"We are safe from Denson Boyd," Sandoval said a few minutes later, toeing something in the dust among the scattered pieces of rock, splintered boards, and shards of glass.

It was a fancy, red-toed boot. Part of a leg bone protruded from the top.

Lucy took a quick look, then turned her pale face away.

To break the mood, Charvein said. "Tell you what, I'm going to carry buckets of water and fill a couple of these old wooden horse troughs. It's coming up another hot day. When the sun warms that water, we could all do with a good bath. Wash some of the dust and blood out of our clothes, too."

Lucy gave him a wan smile. "My dress is nearly indecent."

"Don't worry, Sandoval and I will stay in the cavern until you're done."

"I have a clean shirt," Sandoval said. "If you don't mind man's clothing, I will cut off a pair of my pants. Might come close to fitting you."

"Thank you."

"I had much time to fill," Sandoval added. "I made lye soap from wood ashes and animal grease. I'll find several squares of it while you haul the water."

TWENTY-SIX

Four days later, Charvein was tugging at the packsaddle rope on Sandoval's burro. "I don't know how to throw a diamond hitch, but I reckon this'll hold well enough." He glanced at Sandoval. "Wish you were coming with us."

"I'm still a wanted man in Virginia City," Sandoval reminded him.

"Surely not after what's happened here."

A sardonic smile crossed Sandoval's beardless face. "Would you like to explain all this to the law?"

"Guess you're right. We have a long ride ahead—plenty of time to come up with a plausible story for the sheriff and Ezra Pitney. Have to give 'em a general idea of what happened. But I'll leave out a lot of details nobody needs to know. The bald-faced truth is just too fantastic."

"I'll write it all down in my journal and keep it locked away," Lucy said. "This is better than any tale of knights and ladies."

The three of them had rounded up Boyd's two mules. The animals were now fed and rested, ready to carry Charvein and Lucy back across the playa to Carson City, and on north to Virginia City.

"Thanks for the supplies," Charvein said. "I've packed enough food for the trip. And those kegs of water should be plenty for us and the animals."

Sandoval stroked the nose of his burro. "You may think you have enough water. But don't be doing a lot of washing until you get home."

"You are staying in Lodestar?" Lucy asked.

"Only until my arm heals enough to travel. Beyond that, *quien sabe*? If anyone asks, you can truthfully say you don't know," Sandoval replied. He took off his straw hat, tucked it under the sling of his wounded arm, and wiped his face with his sleeve. "My reason for coming here lies buried up in that graveyard. Buck Rankin and my past—both dead. Time to turn toward another horizon—before someone else comes here, asking many questions."

"You have money?"

He nodded. "I saved a couple gold bars and will finish melting them into small nuggets. As you know, my needs are few. What I kept, I earned."

"Call it a 'finder's fee,'" Charvein agreed.

Charvein held Boyd's mule for Lucy to mount awkwardly from the right side, sparing her wounded leg. In place of the ruined dress, she wore an old shirt and pair of cropped pants that had belonged to the slender Sandoval.

Charvein turned to him. "You know the owner of that gold will be coming to dig up those bell clappers, and the gold cross inside the altar."

Sandoval nodded.

"It's good you smelted the ingots into another form. No exact accounting can be made."

"The works of Providence are many and varied."

"As soon as we're out on the playa, you'll be hard at it

with a shovel, excavating that gold," Charvein said with a wry grin. "Perhaps I should stay a day or two longer and dig it up. But I doubt your little burro, strong as he is, could carry another hundred pounds. If Ezra Pitney comes here and doesn't find it, I'll very likely go to jail for theft."

Sandoval shook his head, somberly. "No need, amigo. My arm will not allow me to dig. Besides, I give you my word I will not touch it. That yellow metal has done its work. Without its help to buy supplies, I could not have survived here four years. And its presence was the means of exorcising my own devil. Now I am a free man."

Charvein shook his head slowly. "You won't be a free man long if you're not telling the truth. I know Pitney. He finds that gold gone, he'll hire the Pinkertons to track you to the end of time."

The bronze face relaxed. "Ah, Señor Charvein, you must really work at having more faith in your fellow man."

Charvein stepped forward and embraced his lean friend in a one-armed hug, avoiding the wounded shoulder. "Is there nothing about Lodestar you'll miss?"

Sandoval looked at the pile of rubble that had been the church. He blinked away a hint of mist in his dark, hooded eyes. "My wife's grave. And . . . the wind ringing the Angelus, day and night—at all the wrong times."